Some of Doc's Blues

Steve Hallock

Pocol Press

POCOL PRESS
Published in the United States of America
by Pocol Press
6023 Pocol Drive
Clifton, VA 20124
www.pocolpress.com

Publisher's Cataloguing-in-Publication

Names: Hallock, Steven M., author.
Title: Some of Doc's blues / Steve Hallock.
Description: Clifton, VA: Pocol Press, 2017.
Identifiers: ISBN 978-1-929763-77-1 | LCCN 2017956078
Subjects: LCSH Musicians--Fiction. | Blues musicians--Fiction. | Jazz musicians--Fiction. | Aging--Fiction. BISAC FICTION / General
Classification: LCC PS3608.A54843 S66 2017 | DDC 813.6--dc23

Library of Congress Control Number: 2017956078

For Maza

The man's voice was raspy, cracked from age and cigarettes and years of gabbing and laughing, as he approached Doc with a request.

"You know what I'd like to hear, Doc." The man grinned.

"'Satin Doll,' Earl?"

Earl winked. "Yep." The neon lights behind the bar reflected off his greasy black hair that was combed straight back. He took a crumpled dollar bill out of his pocket, pulled it straight between his index and middle fingers and dropped it into the tip jar.

Maggio's was packed the last night Doc played the dinner and late drinking crowd before he became famous. Between the tangy homemade tomato sauce and Doc's electric guitar, Maggio's was one of the city's trendier weekend spots. Jazz wasn't Doc's favorite, or best, format, but it helped the digestion and soothed the drunken and forlorn souls. And it was what Maggio paid him to play.

James "Doc" Blevins sat on his stool in the corner of the room, his pick in his teeth while he screwed the G string sharper. He flipped the switch on his rhythm machine, adjusted the dial and tuned in a slow brush snare swing beat. He played the intro to the classic, then moved into a supporting chord, switching from melody to rhythm, bending over his guitar like a seamstress over her machine as he followed the steady hiss of the electronic snare while the chatter of the restaurant crowd hung in the air.

Behind him, a big screen television filled a portion of the wall like a modernistic painting come to life, an arena-full of baseball fans producing a low, steady buzz while the two announcers discussed the benefits of throwing a sliding curve ball when the batter is expecting straight fast stuff.

"Always keep the batter off guard," one voice murmured just below Doc's lead riff.

"Sure. But when your strength is the fast ball, and you're trying to close down an important divisional rivalry, you go with

1

your strongest pitch, and if they hit it, well, you've offered your best."

Doc looked up in mid-tune. Earl stared at him through thick, black-rim glasses. His eyes were moist. The wrinkles in his face held the dim shadows of the bar. He was smiling at Doc, watching the music that came out of Doc's small amplifier. When the song was over, he came out of his seat, walked toward Doc's little stage and, with drink in hand, sat down at the end of the bar, facing the television set behind Doc.

Doc finished his tune and laid his guitar across his lap.

"Know where I first heard that song, Doc?"

Doc knew the story, like he knew the stories of all the bar regulars. But he knew he would have to hear it again anyway. He smiled at Earl. "I'll bet it was the first time you were laid."

Earl grinned. "My mother used to play it when I was a kid. She played it all the time. That and anything else by Ellington." He chuckled and spit a fleck of pasta onto the red carpet. "And Dorsey. And Miller. She'd play those old records of hers in the morning while I was getting ready for school. One time I came out of the bathroom and there she was in the kitchen, movin' around the floor by herself, her eyes closed, like she was dancing." He started to laugh again, but it caught in his throat and became a gurgly cough.

Ed Maggio poked his head out of the kitchen. He glanced at Doc, then at Earl. He pulled his head back into the kitchen, like a turtle withdrawing into its shell. But the look had sent the message. It was the bartender's job, not Doc's, to listen to the sob stories and autobiographies.

"See how this feels." Doc played a couple of be-bop riffs and moved into "'S Wonderful." He played it fast and happy.

"Ah." Earl sighed. "Just what the doctor ordered. You're good, Doc."

Doc's fingers jumped the gaps between strings, landing accurately on each one, spanning frets for the bar chords that lingered and filled in the spaces between the melody notes. He strummed and jabbed and poked the neck of the guitar, evoking bass notes and major sevenths and lead runs out of the instrument.

2

Back in a corner of the restaurant, a young couple got up from their table, their plates half-full of spaghetti and red sauce, their wine glasses nearly drained, and they did a nifty little jitterbug next to the back wall. Doc's jazz, the clinking of glasses behind the bar, the clang of pots in the kitchen, couples talking and making plans for the rest of the night and then the rest of their lives, waiters and waitresses taking orders and setting plates piled with noodles, salads and bowls of soup onto the tables – the noisy restaurant sound track filled Maggio's.

Doc ended the piece with a flourish, just ahead of the baseball announcer's baritone voice exclaiming: "Strike two, he's one and a third innings away from ending this thing."

A couple of people at the bar applauded softly. Doc smiled at them. He motioned to Peggy Maggio, behind the bar, for a glass of beer.

"That was wonderful, Doc. Real nice. I'm heading outside for a smoke."

Earl pulled a pack of cigarettes from his jacket pocket, tapped one out and offered it to Doc. The guitarist shook his head.

Earl grinned. "A guitar player who don't smoke. But I knew that. Thought I'd offer anyway." Earl laughed. "Some things don't change, Doc. You're one of them. And that's a good thing." Earl drained his martini glass, turned to the man next to him at the bar, offered the cigarette to him. The man took it and they stood up, heading outside like two high school kids sneaking a smoke on the parking lot between classes.

Now come the stories. They'll stand outside and talk of the songs they listened to in their youth and how they don't make songs like that anymore. The kind of songs strummed for the dinner crowd at Maggio's, and goddamit anyway, why do we have to get old and all the good songs go away? Doc sighed. Same old chords, same old good songs, week after week.

The ball game ended. The bar customers started working harder on their drinking. Doc drank down half his beer, felt the sudsy cool drink go down his throat, into his gut, then played some easy swing as the early-evening diners and families gave way to the second shift – the older, late-night crowd, the ones with children grown and gone and they'd rather go out than knock around an empty house with each other. The ones who had stayed home early in the evening putting down cocktails to help erase their days from their minds before settling in for a big dinner and a bottle or two of wine. The ones who dropped fives and tens into the tip jar for a little guitar riff from "When Sonny Gets Blue" or "Send in the Clowns." The ones who lingered over a plate of pasta for an hour, pushing the noodles around their plates between drinks and gabbing, waiting – for life to come along.

They were the reason Maggio smiled about 9 o'clock at night, when they started trickling in, filling up their regular tables and bar stools like downtown commuters claiming their same parking spots every weekday morning, ordering the best meals on the menu, followed by dessert and a few drinks.

Doc was the maestro of the night crowd, the reliable music machine.

Doc sat down at the bar for a plate of spaghetti. He faced the TV screen, where a blonde woman with a big, red 0 of a mouth read the day's news. Peggy shoved him a glass of beer to wash down a piece of limp garlic bread.

"Lunch break?"

Doc looked up. A woman stood at the end of the bar, between him and his guitar. He peeked around her, saw his red guitar leaning against the amp, then looked into her face. He smiled. "Hey Louise."

She had watched his eyes go from the bar to the small stage to her. "It's always that damned guitar first, ain't it Doc. The guitar. Then who, or what, after the guitar?"

"Guess that's what I'm waiting to find out Louise, if there's life after music." He shrugged. "I get nervous someone's gonna knock it over, that's all. We get a lotta drunks in here. Someone thinks he played the guitar in some past lifetime and next thing I know he's picking it up and running his fingers across my strings, puttin' it out of tune. That" – he pointed at the guitar – "is my living."

"Okay. But what the hell's your pleasure?"

Doc smiled again. He looked at the plate of spaghetti on the bar, at the half full mug of beer.

"How late do you play?"

"Same as usual, Louise. I got one more set after I eat. Take care of the late night love birds and drunks."

"Then where?"

Doc did a quick study of Louise's face, the rouge brushed softly over the cheeks, the wrinkles that ran out of the corners of her eyes, the mouth in a natural frown that continued down in a furrow toward her chin. She looked alright in the dark. But there are reasons bar owners dim the lights. Everybody looks better in low light, after a couple of drinks. Doc smirked at himself in the mirror behind the bar – his hair still had some blonde in it, combed straight back in waves over his ears and down to his shirt collar. He had wrinkles that Vicki called character lines.

He looked fiftyish. A young fiftyish. Hell. In this place he even looked a decade younger than his 56 years.

"Then, I don't know," Doc said to Louise. "Guess I'm waitin' for that to come along."

"I make a hell of a dessert."

"Maggio doesn't want me mixin' with the customers."

"Oh. That's right. Company policy. I keep forgetting that one."

"Look, Louise." Doc drank the last of his beer and stood up from the bar.

"It's like I've told you before. I think you're a damned attractive woman. You got good taste in music. I'm flattered. But. You know."

"Yeah. But." Louise emptied her glass, leaving a red smudge on its rim. She glanced at the guitar. "What do you do, fuck that thing?"

Doc shook his head. "I guess what I do is my own business, Louise. Good seein' ya." He started for his stool.

Louise grabbed his arm, grasping his bicep with her fingers. "I'm sorry Doc.

I get lonely. Then I start drinkin' and I get crazy. I think you play a hell of a guitar."

Doc smiled into her hazy eyes. "That's okay." He kissed her cheek, and Louise slid into his bar seat. She held up two fingers to Peggy, crossed her legs under her blue skirt and settled in for Doc's last set.

5

Doc found a couple of requests written on scraps of paper on top of his amplifier. He did a quick tune-up, flashed a smile to the room, taking inventory.

About twenty people, most of them couples, most of them caught in conversation, or staring at the big moving picture on the wall. A few solos sat quietly at the bar, peering down into their drinks at some lost fantasy.

He strummed a couple of chords and eased into Jimmy Rushing's and Count Basie's "Blues in the Dark."

At a table for two in the center of the restaurant, an old guy with a gray moustache and a blue blazer bit into a square of garlic toast and chewed on it like a wad of gum. He glanced at the silver-haired woman in flashing spectacles next to him. His hand went into hers. They smiled at Doc, and he nodded to them. This song would probably bring a ten spot his way. He bent over his guitar, plucked out some blues for the old couple.

Doc's fingers were fluid tonight. Sometimes, it took a little work to limber them, to move them along the strings. Sometimes he had to coax the music out of his guitar; it was a moody instrument – like a woman, he used to say – some nights cold and hard, others warm in his hands, nestling into the palm of his hand, the strings almost reaching for his fingers as they wandered along the notes. Tonight, the music came easily.

As the waitresses began laying down the last checks of the night, Doc played the Gershwin brothers' "The Man I Love." He gave it a jazzy, cool reading. While the busboys cleared away dishes holding thin, watery ponds of spaghetti sauce, he bent a bluesy "All My Life" out of the guitar. He could hear the clink of change at the wait station, where the waitresses counted their tips while he did a moody "Prisoner of Love."

The lights blinked on. Louise was gone; he hadn't noticed her leave. A man wandered over from the bar and stuck a crisp dollar bill into Doc's tip jar.

"You play nice." He turned around and walked out the door.

"Thanks." Doc leaned his guitar against the amp, turned off the juice and stood up, stretching out like a man just rising at 6 a.m. from a long, full sleep.

Peggy set a beer on the bar in front of Doc; he spilled out his tips, counted a couple bucks worth of change and tossed it into Peggy's tip jar, then wadded the bills and stuffed them into his pocket.

A waitress vacuumed the carpet. All the lights glared, and the candles were blown out. Drink and sauce stains spotted the beige table cloths and blue carpeting. Doc squinted into the mirror behind the bar, at himself, tall and thin; at the bustle behind him as wives and cooks and busboys hustled to clean up the place and go home to their husbands and televisions and books and stereo systems and lovers and whatever the hell it is people do with their lives at the end of the night. Maggio turned up the volume on the house speakers, filling the room with some Dave Brubeck.

"Nice tunes tonight," Maggio said. He came out of the kitchen, his apron flung over his shoulder like it was a white mink stole tossed there casually by a society dame who put it on as a last thought before going out for the night.

"It's an easy house," Doc said. "I mean, the people are here eating anyway, y'know? I just give 'em some stuff they want to hear, to help their appetites and digestion. Mood music, we call it. Next best thing to Muzak."

"Doc."

"Yeah?"

"I just wish you'd give 'em a little more of the music and a little less of the gab. Peggy does real good with the gab. I know. I live with her.""Yeah. Well sometimes I wish you'd put a little more garlic in your sauce."

"I'll see you later." Doc gently laid his guitar in the case, zipped it shut, flung it over his shoulder and left the restaurant.

Outside, the air had a slight chill. The restaurant's exhaust fan spewed the aroma of garlic and fried sausage and tomato sauce into the night air. The smell clung to the red brick building. Soft yellow light seeped through the windows that made a clear belt around the waist of the building. Paul Desmond saxophone notes pushed through the cracks of the door, climbed out of the stove pipe and gathered in the parking lot like drifting dust.

Maggio had good taste in music, Doc had to grant him that.

A sign rose out of the asphalt and cement and chrome into the dark air, standing among the stars dimmed to a glittering dust by the city lights, proclaiming in red neon letters: "Maggio's Fine Italian Cuisine." Below it, in black letters on a white background: "The doctor is in Thu-Sat nites."

Doc stood under the sign, pulled the wad of bills from his pocket and counted them. Twenty-seven. Plus the hundred bucks Maggio paid him a night. For three hours of work, starting at 7 o'clock and ending around 10. About forty bucks an hour. Doc grinned. Not bad. But no benefits. He gave Maggio's weekly check, three hundred bucks, to Vicki to help with rent and groceries. The tips and what he brought in for odd-job gigs sitting in around town were his. He arranged the money with the ten dollar bill on the bottom, then the five, and then the ones.

He hadn't seen who dropped the ten into the jar; they'd taken care of about a third of his tips for the night. Louise had put in the fiver.

Maggio's neon lights winked off. Doc folded the money and stuffed it back into his pocket. He liked the feel of it there, instead of in his wallet. He liked to stick his hand in his pocket and to touch the money, to know it was right there.

Wouldn't it be nice, he thought as he walked across the parking lot and put his guitar onto the back seat of his car, wouldn't it be something if there was some way to figure out what song sends these old restaurant diners and bar stool denizens to their wallets. Wouldn't it be nice if he knew, for example, who had laid the ten on him tonight, and for what song? Or even, maybe, for a single chord.

Maybe it was just an A minor 7 coming right after a simple G, and it touched some guy right in the heart, like it was a chord progression the guy had heard on the radio a long time ago when he was on a date and fell in love and this song came on the radio, and whenever he hears this chord he remembers that date and how happy he was that night. If you could only figure out what chords hit certain people that way when they came into the restaurant, you could play all the right songs and make a lot of tips.

Just like punching buttons on a car radio set.

Doc climbed into his car, rolled down the window to let in the cool night air, then drove off in search of a six pack of beer and then to the Century Sky Room over on the south side of town.

A drizzle misted the air, blurring the traffic lights and neon signs of the bars and shops. Cars splashed through water that gathered in puddles along the gutters and at the intersections. A street lamp shone down on Doc as he stood on the corner of the convenience store parking lot, a telephone receiver in one hand, a can of beer in the other. He swallowed gulps of beer in between sentences.

"About 30 bucks," he said. "Of course I ate. Don't I always eat? You always remember the times I don't eat, but that hardly happens."

He smiled and listened, rolling cold beer in his mouth like he was sampling a taste of wine before dinner.

"Yeah. So, you comin' to the club tonight? What?" He gestured at the rain clouds with his right hand, grasping the cold beer can like it was a baton and he was conducting the storm. Rain drops sparkled in his hair. He spoke deliberately. "Let me understand this. You prefer some old Woody Allen movie that you've already seen a thousand times to a night at the club with me. Oh sure. Oh sure. I get it."

Doc swallowed more beer and laughed. "Sure, babe. I know you do. I'm only kiddin'. I should be home about 2. We'll get some breakfast in the morning. Yeah. I do you, too." He hung up the phone and stood in the light rain. It ran down the side of his beer can. He put the can to his lips and drank down the rest of it, crunched it like an empty cigarette pack in his hand and tossed it into the trash can next to the entry to the convenience store. He climbed into his car, reached into the back seat and unhooked another beer from the plastic holder. He popped it open and sighed.

Christ. Sometimes I might as well be married, he thought. He started the car. Some BB King guitar licks came on the radio. The heater whirred, gusting cool air across the front seat. Inside the store, a kid with shiny black hair aimed an electronic gun at a black screen, where purple and red and yellow dots zipped up and down and across some imaginary space void. At the counter, a woman with scraggly blonde hair, wearing shorts over dimpled legs and a light jacket on top, handed the clerk a bill. She carried a newspaper and stuck a fresh pack of cigarettes into her jacket pocket. The clerk counted back some bills and change.

It adds up, Doc thought. Just like tips. Rain drops rolled down the window glass. The night he met Vicki was like this one. She had stopped in the restaurant with some friends. They were on the way home from a night on the town, stayed to listen to Doc and his guitar, and after his final set offered to buy him a drink. It was storming outside, a slow night at the restaurant.

She wasn't that much to look at in the dark, that first time. She wore glasses.

Her hair was short, like women cut it when they think they're too old to wear it hanging down to their butts anymore. But from the minute he sat down at the table to gab with her and her friends, she didn't take her eyes off of him. While the other two women talked and joked and surveyed the bar, she listened to Doc's little stories about some of the characters, the regulars, who came into the bar and sat in the same place and ordered their drinks and listened to his music, stories about how the man and wife who owned the restaurant didn't know jazz from rhythm and blues but felt they owed it to the cause of nightlife and restaurants and customer satisfaction in general to provide decent live music.

"And I'm pretty decent live music," he said, leaning across the table to Vicki.

"You play quite well," she said, like it was a fact and not praise.

He liked that. He liked that she didn't fawn over him like some of the drunks who came in and told him he played well even on an off night when he knew he didn't. He liked how she crossed her arms on the table and listened to him intently.

And when the lights came on, and she and her friends had stayed, he liked that she looked even better, with the flecks of gray in her brown hair, the cheek bones that were high and strong, the small gold balls that hung from her ears. She was a nurse; he liked that she cared for people.

11

"How can you be going home this early?" he said as Vicki and her friends began to gather their jackets. "I thought you were out for a night on the town."

"We've been bar hopping since right after work," Vicki said. "That's almost five hours of night on the town. Two of us have baby sitters."

"Are you one of the two?"

She shook her head.

He took her to the Century Sky Room after Maggio's that night. She sat at a small round table two rows back from the stage while Doc sat in with the house band.

She folded her arms and leaned forward, watching the band, like she had listened to him at the restaurant. Doc played a three-chord, 12-bar shuffle behind Ham Grady, who took the sax lead on "Kansas City." Grady dropped the horn from his mouth and stepped aside as Doc ran through a be-bop solo, prying a honky-tonk yelp from his guitar. He strummed the closing E chord and bowed to the applause.

"A little different than what you do at the restaurant," Vicki said when he sat down.

"A lot different." Doc smiled. "That's just my living. This is where I play what I really like."

"You mean they don't pay you for this?"

Doc shook his head. "No. I'm just jammin'. Grady, the tenor man up there, we know each other from way back. I've got an open invitation to sit in."

Vicki looked around the room. It was two-tiered, with red naugahyde booths along the back and side walls, where men in coats and ties and women in red and white and blue evening dresses sat with cigarette holders and glasses of red and white wine that glowed in the soft light. Almost everybody was black, except for Vicki and Doc and a couple of other white faces scattered through the Friday night crowd. The stage, with banks of speakers and amplifiers on each side like giant bookends, dominated the front center of the room. A spotlight cut through the smoke and landed in a big white ball in the center of the stage, where Grady was picking up his tenor saxophone.

Doc tapped Vicki's arm. "This is his gig," he said, motioning to Grady.

"Does he get paid?"

Doc grinned. "Yeah." He looked around at the audience. "He and his band get a salary, plus a percentage of the door. He's makin' a little money tonight."

Vicki put her hand to her lips. "Sshhh." She leaned forward as Grady eased into a breathy "September Song," with Mo Hawkins sliding the brushes on the snare behind him. Doc watched as Vicki ran her index finger along the rim of her wine glass, as she studied the band. She looked over and caught him staring. Her face flushed for a moment, then she turned back to the band. The whole place was quiet except for the clinking of glasses at the bar and some dude at the back, talking in a soft, low monotone that mimicked the searing bass line laid under the song by Goldie Banks.

They went to Vicki's place after the club closed. She made scrambled eggs and toast, and he studied her collection of rock 'n' roll and folk records, and they laughed at some of the old album covers she had carried around since she'd been a teenager. They stayed up most of the night talking. He had talked, anyway.

That was what had drawn Doc to Vicki from the beginning, and it was how he pictured her in his mind whenever he thought of her. Vicki was just what every musician needs. She was a listener. The rain lifted. Doc pulled into the Century Sky Room parking lot, which was wet and shiny like a slick, glossy photograph. Puddles reflected the bent neon beer signs that invited people inside like electric welcome mats. Thousands of raindrops beaded up on the cars that spilled out of the parking lot and onto the street. Groups of two and three people stood on the pavement, cigarettes glowing, their murmuring conversation mingling with the hum of the electric bass that seeped out of the walls. It was a parking lot cocktail party. Doc grabbed his guitar case and walked across the lot.

"Bucko," he said to the doorman.

The big man, his face wet with sweat and rain, smiled. "Go ahead in, Doc. Glad to see ya." He extended his hand.

Doc took the hand and returned Bucko's firm grasp. The only way into the Century Sky Room was past Bucko, a former university linebacker who required a handshake from all men entering his gate.

"I can tell a lot about a person by his handshake," he told Doc once, out on the parking lot between sets. "I can feel who's uptight and wants to fight. I can feel who's mellow and just wants to groove." He winked at Doc. "And I know how to shake hands. You never feel me squeeze yours hard, Doc. That's 'cause I know you're a guitar player and need your fingers. And I know you don't cause trouble." He smiled. "But ask some of those other dudes about my handshake. My handshake tells 'em I'm not to mess with. It's my calling card."

Bucko had blown out a knee a couple of years before during a pro camp tryout. He'd been working at nightclubs ever since, taking day classes to finish up a business degree, fine-tuning his handshake at night. Grady had told Doc about one night that Bucko took a six-inch knife in the arm during a parking lot brawl. But usually, his size was enough to ward off trouble, and there was another one just as big waiting tables inside.

Doc took his guitar case to the side of the stage and pulled out his red Gibson. He blew a puff of hot breath onto a smudge below the E string and buffed the old guitar with the sleeve of his shirt. Grady winked at him and blew his sax like a foghorn, signaling to the rest of the musicians to gather at the stage for the next set. "Can you use a guitar player tonight, buddy?" Doc half shouted to Grady, who was tapping his finger on the microphone to check the sound.

Grady frowned, looking over at Doc like he was some fresh kid just new in the club. "Can you play, white boy?"

"Can I play?"

The two musicians repeated the same game every time.

"Can I play?" Doc stepped up onto the stage and hooked his guitar into the amplifier, strummed a slow, bluesy D9 chord and ran up and down the A minor pentatonic scale a couple of times.

"He can't play. Kick him out." Elaine Barnes, the owner of the club, cackled at a front table. She held a cigarette in her right

14

hand; spent butts filled the small glass ashtray in the center of her table.

Mo Hawkins and Goldie Banks slipped onto the stage. Grady nodded at Doc, tapped his foot on the carpeted stage four times, and the ensemble fell into a slow "Stormy Monday Blues." Grady took the lead, blowing juicy, raspy notes above the vibrating bass. Doc filled the gaps with a progression of chords. That was the thing about the blues. You could do it with three basic chord repetitions, nice and simple. Or you could make it sound so different with just a change in timing or rhythm or phrasing. Or you could jazz it up with a bunch of variations and throw in some be-bop runs and show off for a while.

Doc took his 12 bars and showed off. His fingers danced from the upper string to the bottom as he played a wailing blues litany.

"My, my the man can play, yes," Elaine said. She took a drink of white wine and swirled it in her mouth as Grady answered Doc's solo with a barking, upper-register excursion, lifting his golden bell toward the ceiling like a lonely dog baying at the moon.

The two musicians traded 12-bar licks a couple more times. Banks caressed his bass with his left hand like it was the fragile neck of a woman he loved. His right hand plucked the thick, vibrating strings, coaxing a heavy bass line out of the big-bellied instrument. Hawkins snapped a clean swing on the snare and rang a clear, sharp ting out of the ride cymbal.

"Yeah." Elaine screeched. "Oh, yeah baby." Her black hair fell from the middle of her head in sheets that flowed over her shoulders. Her face was pale; she was like a black and white photograph except for the stark red of her lips and fingernails.

Next to her, a thin kid clutched a creamy white electric guitar. He stood quietly, watching the jam, his lips firm and straight. He wore blue jeans that were tight on his long legs. A piece of silver dangled from his right ear lobe, flashing in and out of the shoulder-length black hair. His arms were lean and muscular in his purple tank-top shirt.

Grady and Doc brought "Stormy Monday" home with a chord flourish, and Hawkins thumped the tune dead. Someone at the back of the room whooped, and applause filled the place. Doc stood his guitar against the amp and headed for the bar, where Mo had a tall glass of beer drawn and waiting.

Page Warner stepped up out of the audience and took his Friday night spot behind the electric piano. Grady went to the microphone. "That was the blues doctor," he said. "He'll be back. Don't worry." He smiled a big, wide grin. "This is the Friday night jam. We like to bring you nine-to-five cats down here once a week to keep your chops. C'mon up here. We welcome a challenge, don't we boys?" He turned and looked at the bass and drum players, who stared straight ahead. "Keep us honest. I see a lot of players out there, so don't be shy."

The kid with the white guitar strode forward and stepped onto the stage.

He whispered into Grady's ear. Grady nodded, turned around to the band and quietly gave some instructions. The kid stared down at the neck of the guitar, watching his fingers chord up and down the frets in a soft Wes Montgomery riff, and then he broke into a trot, picking easily, popping jazz lyrics from the strings. Hawkins and Banks picked up the rhythm, moving with the kid in a loping swing and walking bass. The boy smiled at his guitar. He played easily, grimacing at a blues riff, chording and plucking naturally as he watched his hands on the guitar, like it was just him and the instrument and nobody else in the place.

Doc chugged the beer and motioned to Mo for another. He squeezed between the bar and the tables to the bathroom. Inside the small room, he stood in front of the tiny mirror that was cracked lengthwise down one side. He looked at the sweat that had gathered in the grooves of his face. He showed his teeth in the mirror and smacked his lips.

A man came out of the stall. "H'lo Doc," he said.

"Hey. How's it goin'?"

"It's goin'. The weekend's here." The man smiled.

"I dig."

"You sounded real good up there, Doc."

"Thanks."

"Stop by my table, I'll get you a drink." The man left Doc in the bathroom. Doc stood over the urinal, listening to the muffled

16

music that seeped in through the thin walls and door. The room smelled like stale piss. He zipped his pants, ran his hands under the faucet and glanced at himself in the mirror one last time as he dried. Fuck. How long ago had he been that kid up on the stage, ready to blow away all the old farts and claim his title as the new young blues king? It was like another lifetime. Someone else's lifetime, somewhere else, when there still was enough time to do it right.

He had a fresh beer waiting for him when he got back, with a side shot of Jim Beam.

The kid guitarist, his white instrument flashing in the dim bar, glanced toward Doc, then down at his guitar. He pulled a long, whining train wail out of his strings, bending the train whistle up and down the tracks. Then he stopped. The room held its breath. He repeated the wail, stretching the note into an amplifier feedback, then stopped again. The room counted: One, two, three, four, and the musicians jumped into "The Train Kept a Rollin'." The kid's fingers sped up and down the neck of the guitar like train yard gandydancers at quitting time as he took the lead. He stepped to the microphone. "Get along, sweet little women, get along."

His voice was high and sharp. Strong, and thin, like the boy. His guitar echoed his voice.

"And the train kept a rollin', all night long;

"And the train kept a rollin', all night long."

Hawkins played the drums at fast train tempo, clicking his sticks on the snare like wheels moving along the tracks. Banks had switched to an electric bass; he chugged and huffed at the bottom of the tune, pulling it along, filling the club with a deep, diesel bass line. The boy guitarist was all up and down his guitar now, barreling through the rock/boogie at breakneck speed, until he suddenly pulled up and signaled the band to a halt. The room echoed for a moment like a train station reverberating with the clack of a departing freight. The guitarist smiled, looked up at the crowd, then back at his guitar.

"Oh, my mama!" someone yelled.

The kid yanked one more train whistle out of his guitar, a long, groaning, meow of a lament, then a roar of a blues, then a strum of a chord, which he dropped off string by string, moving back into a single-string moan that disappeared into the distance, softer, ever softer, until it was gone.

Half the room, mostly the younger crowd, jumped up in applause. The guitarist nodded at the audience. He smiled at Doc, who picked up his beer glass and drained it. Doc gave the kid a grin, set his empty glass on the bar and went back to the stage. The kid yielded.

"Worry, Worry, Worry," Doc said to Grady. The sax player chuckled and turned to set the rhythm players. Doc rested his guitar on the small paunch of his belly and waited.

A layer of chatter filled the room. Still talking about the young guitar player. Doc wiped the back of his arm across his forehead and watched Grady. The horn player nodded at the guitarist.

Suddenly Doc shot a couple of fast blues licks, loud and sharp, through the room. He sprayed the audience with blues bullets, aiming his guitar from left to right, pulling on the strings like they were triggers on a blues gun. Then, just as suddenly, he backed off and, cradling his guitar into his body, moved into a lyrical, slow blues. Hawkins rolled the snare gently behind Doc while Grady lay down sedimentary layers of support notes beneath Doc's sad guitar.

Doc dropped his right hand to his side, moving his left fingers slowly up and down the frets as he approached the microphone. His droopy, sad eyes scanned the room, landing on Ma. She stood behind the bar, a glass of red wine in her hand, watching him.

"Oh, worry worry worry," Doc sang each vowel like it was a guitar string. "Worry is all I can do."

"I'll say." Elaine stretched her legs into the aisle, toward the stage. "Sing it, Doc."

Doc grinned at her, picked out a couple of blues notes and tossed them to her.

"Oh, my life is so miserable baby, and it's all on account of you."

"Indeed!" came from the back of the room. Doc smiled while he kept singing. "You hurt me so bad baby, when you said we were through."

Doc stepped back from the mike and repeated the melody he had just sung, stretching the longer notes, turning the musical staff lines into blues rubber. He stepped back to the microphone.

"Someday baby ... someday baby." He waved a finger at Elaine. "Oh yes, someday baby ... ohhhhh yessss, someday baby."

Elaine puckered her lips. "Mmmmmmm. Please." She rasped laughter.

Doc sang. "Mmmm." He moved backward again and strummed a blues so soft as he trilled the E and B strings you could hear the fans blowing the smoke out the open front door. Thunder belched in the distance as a fresh rain storm rolled off the mountains. Doc sent his easy chords skipping out the door and across the city, bouncing up the streets and against the passing cars like blue flood waves. He took a breath, held his hand high above his guitar, then swooped down for the blues finale.

He massaged the guitar, rubbing blues notes out, moving from a fast be-bop, popping-string solo into a chord progression that erected a pyramid of blues in the middle of the room, which he shot down with another blast of machine gun blues, with Hawkins banging out a tom-tom conclusion, Grady squealing and squawking an ad-lib free-form side dish that somehow meshed with Doc's final chord. Thunder cracked the place as the musicians dropped their instruments to dangle like dead birds from their necks. Shouts and applause filled the room, finally giving way to the rain beating a steady tempo on the plexiglass cover of the Sky Room's front porch.

The room took a big gulp of cool air that blew in from the black night. Doc looked across the room at the kid. The boy smiled. He was packing his white guitar into its case. He relinquished the room to Doc and carried his guitar out the door, down the metal stairs and into the parking lot, where raindrops danced to the Sky Room's jukebox.

At the end of the set, Grady and Doc stood on the porch that overlooked the glistening parking lot. The lights of the city were hazy in the distant mist.

"Where's the old lady?" Grady said.

"I think she found a movie on the tube."

"She ain't been comin' around with you much lately."

"Yeah? So where's yours?"

Grady lit a cigarette and blew a line of white smoke toward the parking lot. Inside the bar, the jukebox hummed. Ice cubes tinkled in half-empty glasses. Elaine hacked and coughed laughter. The tables were mostly empty, as the men and women of the bar gathered on the porch and on the steps, down in the parking lot, gasping breaths of the damp air, blowing clouds of smoke into the starless sky. Ray Charles sang on the jukebox: "Hey woman, don't you treat me wrong; come an' love your daddy all night long."

"You blew that kid away," Grady said.

"Uh huh."

"Man, you did." Grady took a drink of rum from his glass. "And you did it with finesse."

"I know." Doc looked at Grady. "I know I did. But the kid's got chops. God he's got chops."

"But you got 'em too. And you got what counts."

"Yeah?"

"Yeah. You feel the music. I don't care how fast anybody plays if he don't play with feeling. You do."

Doc sighed. "I guess. But I'm old, Grady. I'm old, and I know I'm never going anywhere but here. Here, and my restaurant gig."

"So? A lot o' cats don't even have gigs, man. An' you know you got one right here with me anytime you want it. A payin' gig. Can't beat that. Man, put your crowd together with mine and together we can own this goddam town. Not many players who can say that."

On the parking lot, a man and a woman embraced next to a shiny black convertible with white naugahyde seats that shone pink in the stormy night air. He was in a black suit. She wore a red gown that clung to her legs and waist. "Maybe that's why you can play like you do," Grady said. "Maybe gettin' old and feelin' the world is part of playin' good."

Doc grinned. "You're full of shit, Grady."

Grady smiled. "Me. I got what I want. You and me, we're the ones who're left tonight. The kid left, you didn't. I didn't. We're here. It's your stage." Grady chuckled.

"Except for when I step up. Then it's all mine, my man."

Thunder rumbled in the mountains. Lightning cut a jagged line in the sky, flickering across the plains. Then the sky was black again.

"Grady."

"Yeah."

"Here's the part that pisses me off. I know I blew that kid away. I know it's my stage."

"Yeah."

A cool wind blew Doc's blonde and gray hair straight back, like the pompadours the cool jazz players used to wear. His silver whiskers shimmered in the night light.

"But he's gonna make it, Grady." He pointed his finger toward the city, jabbing at a glistening skyscraper. "That kid's gonna make it. He's good. He's gonna take everything he's learned from me and you, the blues, jazz, technique, he's gonna take it all and make some money at it. He's gonna ball all the women and play all the notes and put it all in the bank."

"Fine." Grady carried his empty glass inside and sat down next to the stage. He shouted back to Doc. "Fine. But you still blew him away. And that's all that matters tonight."

Doc sent a sigh across the parking lot. He watched the men and women on the damp concrete, sucking on their cigarettes, combing their slick hair, listening to the blues and jazz on the car radios, embracing and kissing.

Ray Charles finished his song. "See the girl with the red dress on; she can do the Birdland all night long."

"Yeah, yeah."

Doc looked inside the bar at Grady, sitting alone at the table. You see a man on a consistent basis over the years, it seems like he doesn't change. Yet here Grady was, a different man than the one Doc knew as a young player, the brash black sax man with the thick, curly hair piled up on his head like a turban, his arms thin and muscular. He looked mean then, with a goatee and moustache that gave him a permanent scowl, until his face spread into a wide grin after a sax solo that went down like sugar in iced tea.

Tonight, a V of bald skin cut into Grady's closely cut short hair from a forehead folded into wrinkles. His belly hung over his belt buckle. He wore a gray whisper of a moustache. But the smile was the same. And the playing was better than ever.

Grady had stayed in town, building his rep over the years. He put in time backing other musicians, playing other people's gigs, all the time refining his own technique, blowing his horn at home during his off hours, until finally he landed at the Century Sky Room with his own band and staked his musical claim as the most solid sax man in town.

The Century became his club more than a decade ago. Doc had invited him on the road years ago. Grady, married, didn't even think about it. "I can play my music right here with my friends in my town," he said. "You go ahead. And when you come back, I'll still be here. You come in and play with me then."

Doc went inside and sat down with Grady. Ma brought a half-empty bottle of whiskey and a draft of beer and set them in the middle of the table. Doc sucked the suds off the top of the beer and poured himself a whiskey.

"That kid was me up there tonight, Grady."

The sax player nodded. "I know. I saw. I remember how you used to come into a club and blow everybody away with your loud, fast hotshot guitar."

Prince Tower sat at the Century's piano, playing some Oscar Peterson chords. Nobody knew how old Prince was. He had a thin face with tight skin that showed every dip and curve in his skull. His bald head shone softly in the spotlight as he bent over the keys, peering through rimless spectacles. He came out about once a month, and he sat and played a moody piano for a couple of hours, drank a single glass of beer, then disappeared, back to an apartment he shared with an ancient mother, where he wrote page after page of obscure jazz that played only in his mind.

Grady and Doc sat at the table near the door, listening to the rain that had leveled off into a soft, gentle rhythm outside the door and the easy, melodic musings of Prince on the piano. They poured more whiskey.

"I wonder what he's gonna do with it," Doc said.

"Huh? Who?"

"That kid. He's good. I wonder where he's going. Y'know, you only get one, maybe two shots."

"You and me think different," Grady said. "It's all one shot, to me, and I'm still taking it."

"I know. Man, Grady, it wasn't that long ago. Y'know? It wasn't that long ago."

"Drink up, my man. Listen to Prince play. He don't think about these things. He just plays."

"Who knows what the hell Prince thinks about?" Doc grinned at his friend, lifted his whiskey glass in a toast and drank it down.

The clouds broke up about 2 a.m. The stars, glistening clean after the night's shower, filled the air with white dots, like a million quarter notes on a big, black free-form jazz chart.

Doc carried his guitar case down the Sky Room's cement stairway. Couples stranded in the morning between Friday and Saturday clutched each other on the parking lot. Cigarettes glowed. Rain puddles gathered like tiny round mirrors in the parking lot. Car engines rattled.

"G'night, Doc." Grady spoke softly across the parking lot. "Tell Vicki hi."

Doc nodded his head. He watched Grady carefully lay his sax case on the back seat and then climb into the front seat, where he revved the engine a couple of times and tuned his radio dial among talking voices and classic rock. Grady flicked a cigarette lighter that filled his car with a flash of orange. Doc envied Grady's contentment, his steady house gig at the Century Sky Room, which seemed to fill up every night with customers who dug good music and knew how to listen, who spent their money on booze and women. Grady drove an old Ford station wagon that was paid off, he was married to the same woman for more than 30 years. She held a day job as a secretary. They ate dinner together every night before Grady came to the club.

The air smelled new. Doc strapped his guitar to his back, scraped his feet across the parking lot and headed for the all-night coffee shop a couple of blocks away. On the street, headlights

23

flickered in the distance like cat's eyes yawning open and shut in the middle of the night. Streetlamps stood a block apart in a line of light that split open the blackness like a silver zipper. Parking meters lined the side of the street like iron tree seedlings. Doc walked along the sidewalk. Drops of water rolled off the roof, falling into small pools that gathered in the recesses of wet cement. The streetlights, the neon bulbs fronting the small shops, the headlights of passing cars all glowed in the surface of the damp street.

Somewhere, far away, Doc heard the music of a blues band. It came closer and louder, filling the street with a forlorn harmonica, like the lonely whistle of a 3 a.m. train. Then it was on top of him. A creamy, smooth car motored by, its windows down, blaring music from a couple of speakers in the back seat. It turned the corner and was gone, trailing piano and sax notes like exhaust, until the night was quiet again.

He stopped in front of the G.I. Pawn. A Ludwig drum set, surrounded by wide, golden cymbals, sparkled red in the window. Doc remembered George Harper, with the big bass drum that boomed across the football field, the marching toms that George played like the snare and side tom of a trap set. George was going to be a drummer in a big band. He left town the day after he graduated from high school, and nobody heard from him again.

A pang of dizziness hit Doc's head. Too many whiskeys and beers tonight. It happened whenever Prince Tower came in and hogged the piano, so the only thing to do was sit and drink and listen. Doc leaned against a light pole and studied the pawn shop and its shelves of dreams sold cheaply. Computer keyboards that had clicked out first, second, third novels. Sound systems that accompanied painters drenching their canvases in oils. Watches given to 18-year-old high school graduates, pawned by 58-year-old men in drunken stupors.

And the guitars, hung in rows along the wall next to the drum sets, behind the glass counter filled with trumpets and clarinets, hawked for a few bucks – just until their owners got one more band together, just long enough to pay one more month's rent, just for this weekend, man, so's I can buy a sack of groceries.

And finally, the last reason, because I'm fed up with this music shit.

Dig.

Stratocasters, Gibsons, Fenders, Rickenbackers, Tokais, all buffed shiny clean in red, blue, black and silver, beige. Doc wondered how many of them represented the end of the road, traded in for a wedding band or for a few bucks and another round of booze. Next to the electric guitars were the acoustics, blonde, tan, red wood. One of them looked like the guitar Doc's father had given him on his 10th birthday. "Just an option, kid," his father had said. "People who can play music never go hungry."

Grady had said Doc was the best. But that kid tonight was good. God he could play.

The black van quietly drove up behind Doc. It parked. The side door slid open. Then it clicked shut. The van drove away, leaving empty pavement in front of the pawn shop, where a moment before Doc had been pondering failed dreams.

Everything was black when Doc opened his eyes. He heard voices, a man and woman talking, laughing, muffled by a door or wall. He tried to remember this party, when he had arrived, whose house he was at. His eye caught a thin yellow line, light seeping in underneath a door. Someone was drinking and listening to music in the next room. Doc could hear the clinking of ice against glass, the slurp of liquid. He smelled cigarette smoke.

He lay on his back and let his mind roam backwards in time, to The Palmer House Hotel, with its lounge off the alley. As a teenager, he had sat in the parking lot on Saturday nights and watched smoke rush out the door to mingle with the air, gray and steamy. Guitar and saxophone music floated out the open door and drifted into the night.

Men and women sat on waxed car hoods and smooched.

One night a man in a white suit and a woman in a white dress embraced and danced, gliding around the parking lot.

Doc turned on his side and put his arm out for Vicki. It fell through air and bumped against cushioning. His back curled into firm support. He was on a couch. Somewhere outside a truck shifted through gears and motored away. Doc sat up. His head ached. A wave of nausea hit him. He dropped his head back into the pillow.

Sometimes, late at night when he was supposed to be asleep, the boy heard his father at the piano in the living room, pressing his fingers into a series of forlorn chords, humming along to the blues and jazz riffs. Or he would hear his father's radio playing band music. Trumpets blared tinny swing through the scratchy static. But the music he remembered best was a recording his father played of a guitarist named Django Reinhardt. He remembered lying in his bed, sweaty, tossing back and forth beneath the sheets, and then Django's guitar came in chords interrupted by syncopated jazz notes, and the music swept across the boy and out his open window, away into the sky as he fell asleep on a summer night.

A breeze blew across Doc's forehead. He found a window high in the wall at the other end of the room. Blue-gray dusk filled the air.

The boy's father slipped a 78 r.p.m. onto the record player. Sippie Wallace gurgled a throaty "Dead Drunk Blues." Louis Armstrong led the way on the trumpet. The summer night heat gathered in the living room. Miller moths and gnats smacked into the searing, yellow light bulb, and their lives ended with a pppfft. The boy sipped an icy lemonade and watched his father dig the blues.

"Listen to the guitar, son."

The record ended, and his father stuck another on the rotating wheel, carefully lifting the needle arm and setting it down at the beginning of the record. Hot Lips Page coaxed a blues from his trumpet. Tiny Grimes came in from the back of the song, laying down guitar chords for support. The boy held his guitar on his lap. He clumsily fingered the frets. He rubbed his sweaty fingers up and down the strings, squeaking an adolescent blues out of the instrument. His father sat next to the hi-fi, cigarette smoke pluming into the air above him, where it spread out like a dying storm cloud.

The sky beyond the window looked like a gray coat of paint. Drops of water rolled down the glass. The weather reminded Doc of the last night he'd spent with his father. It was a summer night. He and his father sat on the front porch, his father with a can of beer, the boy with a bowl of ice cream. A soft rain fell on the green lawn beyond the porch. The radio was on in the living room.

"Sing, Bessie." The boy's father blew a stream of smoke at the roof. "Yeah."

Bessie sang. "I hate to see, the evening sun go down."

Bwa bwa bwa ba de da de da.

"I hate to see the evenin' sun go down."

His father leaned back against the wooden post that held up the hand rail. He took a long drink of beer.

"St. Louis woman, wears a diamond ring; pulls her man around on her apron string."

Ah, blow that horn.

"Got the St. Louis Blues, yes I'm blue as I can be."

"Sing it, Bessie." His father looked beyond the boy, beyond the porch.

The boy sat with his bowl of ice cream, melted vanilla that was still cool. He lifted the bowl, drank down the sweetness, then watched his old man close his eyes and sip in the blues. Sing it, Bessie. A week later his father was gone. For a couple of days, his mother sat in the living room, staring at the wall, listening to whatever the radio played while she worked through a bottle of clear booze. The boy came in on a Saturday afternoon and found her sitting in the middle of a pile of smashed phonograph records, his father's music.

"He's not coming back," she said. Her eye sockets were dark. Lipstick ran from a corner of her mouth like blood. A half glass of gin sat on the hardwood floor next to her. "He doesn't love me anymore. You neither, I guess."

"Why?"

"He got the wanderlust." She sighed. "I knew it when I married him. He's not capable of settling into a place, bein' a family man. I don't even think it's his fault. He just doesn't have it in him. And you can't change a man." She focused her eyes on the boy. "Except when he's a boy, bein' brought up under the influence of his mother. C'mere."

She took the boy in her arms and held him. He could smell the liquor on her breath, mingling with the sweetness of her perfume. Her tears dampened his cheeks. She pulled back from him and looked into his face.

"You've got his hair, his eyes. Hell, you're him all over. You'll probably be just like him. But that's okay. I'll love you anyway. Just like I do him, dammit all."

The room was bright the next time Doc opened his eyes. He sat up, lifted his legs over the side of the couch and touched the floor. He was fully clothed.

"Geezus." Doc held his head between his hands. He stood up, pulled open the door and went into a small hallway. The bathroom was at the end. He went in, turned on the switch, and an electric fan rattled into motion. Doc hacked and spit into the toilet, unzipped his pants and sighed as he emptied his bladder. It was a bathroom like any apartment bathroom, with white walls and tile, a white tub. A bathroom he had seen a thousand times and one he'd never seen before.

He flushed, bent over the sink and ran some cold water into his mouth, then looked into the mirror. His eyes were red. Gray stubble covered his face.

"Geezus," he mumbled.

A voice came from outside the door.

"Doc?"

It was a woman's voice.

"Doc?"

"Yeah."

"You okay?"

"I think so, yeah."

He studied himself in the mirror, like he was looking at someone else. His head went around. He pressed his hands to his temples, trying to squeeze the hangover out of him.

"Where am I?" he shouted. "Who are you?"

There was no answer. It was like the old days, when there was always a woman waiting after a gig, and he went home with her and woke up the next morning and it took a while to figure out where he was and whom he was with. But he hadn't done that in the last two years or so, not since Vicki. He tried to remember. The pawn shop came at him, with all the guitars. Then somebody was guiding him into a car. They handed him a bottle. The radio was playing. The smell of perfume and cigarette smoke mixed with fresh air that blew through an open window. He drank from the bottle, then some more, then came dark sleep. And here he was with a throbbing head, an aching body and a jumpy stomach.

"Oh shit." Doc jerked the bathroom door open and rushed back to the room where he woke up. He scanned the floor, looked behind a desk, then jerked open a closet door. His guitar case stood in the corner. He took it to the couch, opened it and lifted out the guitar. He sat down and plucked each string, then pulled his fingers across a chord. The guitar was in tune. It was okay.

He let out a sigh.

"Everything alright? Other than what must be a hellacious hangover."

Doc looked up. The voice came from a woman with hair that wavered between deep red and purple and hung in thick waves over her shoulders. She wore a one-piece dress with horizontal black bars on a light pink background. It ended about six inches below her knees, where white stockings took Doc's eyes the rest of the way to the floor and her solid black pumps.

"Who are you? And where am I?"

She crossed the room and handed Doc a cup of coffee. "I'm Saundra. That's long for Sandy, which is what my friends call me. And you're with friends."

"Thanks." Doc looked down into the cup at the hot, black coffee. His stomach jerked. He handed the cup back. "I don't believe so right now."

She sat down on the couch next to him. She carried a scent of lilacs or some kind of perfume Doc recognized from the night before, and from somewhere else.

Then he knew. It was his mother's scent.

"How's the head?" She smiled at him and lifted her eyebrows. Her whole face was a paint job, from the red lipstick to the thick eyelashes.

"It hurts."

"I believe you. You were drunk when we picked you up, and you attacked the bottle I gave you like somebody who's been on the desert without water for a week."

"Yeah." Doc studied her. She watched him, her eyes big and round, waiting for him to say something.

"Where am I? And who are you?"

"You're repeating yourself." She smiled for effect. "You are in a studio office on the east side of town. I am one of your biggest fans."

Doc leaned back and grinned. "Is that all this is? You some kind of groupie and you brought me home last night?"

She stood up. Doc followed her down the hallway into a small living room.

She carried the unwanted coffee into a big kitchen, where an ashtray filled with cigarette butts sat in the middle of a formica dining table. Next to it was a deck of cards and a digital clock that displayed 9:35. The only sound was the whirring of the refrigerator and the occasional splash of a car running through a rain puddle outside.

Computer equipment filled the desk next to the wall between the living room and kitchen. A window looked out onto a brick warehouse. Recording gear, mikes, amps, filled a set of shelves on the wall opposite the window and front door. Doc studied the gear.

He whistled. He'd been in a recording studio, and this stuff was recording studio quality. A pair of loudspeakers stood at each end of the shelves that were stocked with at least two of everything: turntables, old reel-to-reel tape decks, video and audio gadgets, tuners. Dusty stuff, relegated to shelves with the advent of digital computer recording. A big-screen television monitor hung on the wall.

"Maybe this'll suit you better." Sandy came from the kitchen with a can of beer. "There's some truth to what they say about drinking booze to get rid of a hangover. I know."

"I'll bet you do." Doc took the beer, popped it open and went to the window. He took a drink and felt the cold beer flow all the way down to his stomach, where it settled in and started to ease the jitters right away.

He smacked his lips. "Best medicine known to man."

The neighborhood reminded him of the downtown apartment he and his mother moved to after his father left. Next to the red brick warehouse, trash and weed stalks filled a small vacant lot with a foot path through the middle of it. There was a five-story brick apartment house to the left. The streets were nearly bare. A semi cab was parked half a block up. An old green pickup truck spotted with rust sat on the other side of the vacant lot. Empty liquor bottles and broken glass littered the doorway of the warehouse.

The sky was a gray bowl; no telling where the sun was.

Sandy came with a drink of her own and stood next to Doc at the window.

"You're just not going to tell me any more than I ask, are you?" he said.

"Dexter is going to meet us later," Sandy said. "He's my boss. He'll answer all your questions. Believe me, Doc, you're going to like what you hear. You're too talented a man to waste the rest of your life playing the guitar for a bunch of drunks in a restaurant bar and playing for free in downtown dives. That's what this is all about."

"Okay." Doc swished beer in his mouth like it was mouthwash. It tasted good. "But why did you bring me here? I don't get it."

"We were going to take you out for coffee after your gig last night. You slipped out so quickly. We caught up with you a couple blocks later." She stopped and laughed.

"Anybody would've sworn you were some drunken bum. You were standing there – actually, teetering is more like it – in front of that pawn shop, your guitar hanging from your back like a bag of clothes. We stopped, you got in and we headed for an all-night diner. God, Doc, you were gone, mumbling about old guitars and failed hopes. You grabbed the bottle from me and drank it. Hell. We just brought you back here to sleep it off."

"Yeah. Well, I do that once in a while. I usually end up at Grady's place though."

"You can really play, Doc. We've been listening to you, at the restaurant, at the Century. You deserve better."

Doc grinned. "I don't know what your game is, lady, but you've got my attention. Who is this Dexter fellow?"

"He's someone who's going to help you."

"Right. I've heard that before. A little money up front, right? Then stardom and happy ever after tomorrow."

"You'll just have to talk to Dex."

"Yeah. Okay. Meanwhile, I need a shower and some clothes. You and Dexter going to fix that for me?"

She smirked. "Not right now. I'll take you back to your car. But first I want you to promise me something."

"I don't make promises. That way I don't break 'em."

"You do alright for a fellow with a hangover." Sandy wrote something on a piece of paper at the kitchen table and handed it to Doc. "I'd like you to meet me at this club about 8 o'clock tonight. Bring your guitar. We're going to ask you to sit in with a band."

Doc looked at the paper. The name of the club was the Sundial Inn. "This is a cowboy bar. I don't play shitkicker music. Besides. I gotta play my restaurant job tonight."

"Doc." Sandy sighed. She grabbed her purse and took out her billfold. She counted out five twenty-dollar bills. "Here's a night's wages for you. Call in sick."

Doc took the money, folded it in half and stuck it in his shirt pocket.

"How do you know how much I make?"

Sandy shrugged. "Put that on your list of questions to ask Dex tonight. He's calling all the shots. I'm just the hired help. C'mon, I'll drive you to your car."

Doc lay his guitar in one of the back seats and strapped it in with a seat belt. As Sandy merged the van into traffic, he pulled the top off another beer, took a long drink and stuck the cold can between his legs. He watched the neighborhoods pass by the side window. Wes Montgomery played "West Coast Blues" on the stereo speakers that surrounded the front seat. Guitar chords rolled through the carpeted interior of the van. Sandy didn't look like a Wes Montgomery type, though.

Doc pictured her listening to country music.

She pulled into the Century Sky Room parking lot and stopped behind Doc's car. It was alone, surrounded by pavement that was littered with cigarette butts and empty beer cans. The nightclub was a faded pink in the daylight, with a couple of black eighth notes painted on the side, and the words "Century Sky Room" below them.

"See you tonight."

"I'll be there," Doc said.

"With your guitar, honey."

"Right." He hung his guitar over his shoulder and stood in the parking lot to watch her drive away.

He swallowed a gulp of beer and swished it in his mouth while he thought about his situation.

Somehow this didn't seem like the way one went about being discovered as a musician.

It was a different city in the daylight, like what happens to a woman overnight, you wake up and she's familiar but changed.

33

Stacks of cement and glass stood where glistening lights had been the night before. A blue sky, tinged brown with smog, filled the black bowl that had been the night sky. Instead of stars winking at you, puffy white clouds hung in the air like boat sails.

Doc drove across the river, a band of brown water that looked cold and choppy. The cinders and steel tracks of the railroad yards glistened. Then he was out of downtown and driving through the fringe neighborhoods of the city, past old brick homes with covered wooden porches and green lawns, with big oak and elm trees lining the streets and covering gray sidewalks that rocked and rolled, cracking and conforming to the swaying land as it climbed up out of the river valley.

He drove down the alley behind Vicki's place. He still called it Vicki's place, even though they lived together. He sat in his car behind the two-story house and drank the last of his beer. He tossed the empty can into the back seat and took his guitar upstairs.

The place was cool, quiet. It was Vicki's Saturday to work the emergency room. Doc liked this part of the musician's life, the quiet day hours, having the apartment to himself to wander in, now and then strolling through a neighborhood populated only by a few other people who had their daytime hours at home. He liked sleeping until he woke up instead of being jarred out of bed by a blaring alarm. He liked waking up slowly with coffee and the news on the radio while outside, a few blocks away, cars whizzed to and from town on errands, jobs, appointments. He enjoyed starting his working day when most people were ending theirs. If you call playing the guitar work.

Doc went to the bathroom and started a stream of hot water in the tub. He pulled his clothes off, tossed them into the basket Vicki kept in the hallway closet, then found a can of beer in the refrigerator. Vicki always kept him stocked with beer. Doc went back to the steamy bathroom and settled into the tub of hot water. He leaned back, resting his head against the wall behind the tub. He took a long shot of cold beer, and he sighed out loud. Two more drinks, and he nodded into a nap. With the warm water lapping around the red flesh of his legs and stomach, he was a soft, pulpy island rising out of the aqua water that settled into a still

pool around him, rippling gently as Doc snored softly, his right
hand clutching the cold can of beer.

The phone rang. Doc found himself sitting in a tub of cool
water. He stood up and dripped a wet trail into the living room.

"Hello."

"Doc."

"Hey, Vicki."

"You alright?"

"Yeah. Just one of those nights."

"You usually call me. You stay over at Grady's?"

"No."

"Doc?"

"It's a long story, Vicki. I met someone. This woman ..."

"Huh?"

"No. No. She works for this guy."

Doc, who could ad lib his way through any walking blues,
had trouble with this story.

Vicki rescued him.

"Listen. I got another call coming in. Tell me about it
tonight. I just wanted to make sure you got home okay."

"Yeah. But about tonight. I got a new gig I'm supposed to
be at."

"Sounds like you had quite a night. New job. New girl. Will
you be home tonight?"

"Yeah. Sure."

"Good. I'll be home late. Shirley wants me to help her pick
out a dress after work. Talk to you later tonight."

"Look, Vicki," Doc started to tell Vicki it wasn't like she
was thinking, but she'd already hung up. "Dammit," he said as he
walked down the hallway to the bathroom.

Doc imagined Vicki on her phone, in her pale green
uniform, her hair combed neatly, a pencil in her hand, her glasses
perched on her nose like when she was home reading her
magazines, her lips set together tightly. Picture this woman living
with a drunken blues musician, he thought.

He wrapped a towel around himself and took the disposable
razor from the medicine chest. He covered his face with lather and
sliced off a day's growth of whiskers. As a boy, he had watched

his father shave, whether it was before a new part-time piano job in a downtown honky-tonk or for a full-time day job stacking boxes in a warehouse. "People don't want to mess with messy folks," his father said.

He studied the shave job, the web of wrinkles around the eyes, the deeper creases that crossed the forehead. His skin was pink and smooth from the hot water and razor.

He sighed at the face in the mirror. "Nothin' I can do about it. I'm stuck with you no matter what you look like. I guess we've done alright so far."

He left the apartment early. He wanted time to scope the place out over a couple of beers. The address was on the far west side of town, on motel row, where the truckers pulled off at night. Diners and bars filled in the gaps between the motels on the four-lane road that led out of town.

He found the club under a yellow sign in the shape of a sun, with a bunch of spokes coming out all around it. Black letters said it was the Sundial Inn. Behind it, the mountains sliced the real sun in half as it dipped below the jagged horizon for the night. Sundown came early on the west side of town, in the shadow of the hills. Doc parked at the back, next to the dumpster, grabbed his guitar and went inside. He found a wooden booth against a wall near the small stage.

The place was dark. There were a few bodies at the bar, folks getting an early start on the night's drinking. He knew this kind of bar, had played in a hundred like it on the road when he was young. It was not the kind of place where people went to listen to the music.

It was the kind of place where people went for the booze and the noise and to yell and dance and maybe find someone to love for a few minutes in the parking lot at midnight, when you've drunk your pride and discretion away and the air is cold and you're cuddled into someone's arms under the shimmering stars with music playing on the car radio and you're groping and clawing and for a few moments think you've found what you've been looking for. And in that short, happy span of your life, you feel like craning your neck and baying at the moon.

"Hey Doc. You made it." It was Sandy's voice. Doc squinted and peered into the dim light of the club. Sandy came at him from the bar.

"You wanna drink?"

Doc nodded.

"Beer?"

"An' a shot of whiskey."

Sandy went to the bar and ordered drinks from the bartender.

"Mr. Blevins?"

Doc looked up. A pear shaped man with a cowboy hat on the stem end stood between Doc and the front door.

"You know who I am," Doc said, smiling up at the man. "Now make us even and tell me who you are."

"Dexter. Dexter Graham. Mind if I sit down?"

"It's your show."

Sandy brought the drinks to the table. She set a beer and a shot of whiskey in front of Doc and a beer in front of Dexter.

It was an expensive looking cowboy hat, soft white with a thick red band around it, one of those ten-gallon jobs like they used to wear on the old black-and-white westerns on TV. Beneath the hat, Dexter wore a full, black beard. A thick moustache curled over his lip. His eyes were narrow and dark in the low light, so it was hard to study him and get a reading of what might be inside. He wore a small, gold star in his left ear lobe.

Fiddle music and a doo-wop bass came on the jukebox that shone like a camping lantern in a corner of the bar.

"I'm sure you're wondering what this is all about, Mr. Blevins."

Doc smirked. "Gee, Dexter. Am I that easy to figure out?"

The man smiled, and his eyes crinkled. He had a friendly face and a soft voice.

"Okay if I call you Doc?"

"Yeah." Doc threw the whiskey into his mouth and chased it down with a half mug of beer. "I just wish you'd get to the point."

"Alright." Dexter pulled his wallet out of the tweed sport coat he wore over a white dress shirt with pearl buttons that flashed just below the collar of the coat. He held a wad of bills in his hand. "This is the point, my guitar-playing friend."

The bill on the end closest to Doc was a hundred.

"I get it," Doc said. "Look. I've been approached by agents before. This is the first time anyone's gone to so much trouble. Usually they come into the club, offering me the west coast and the east coast and recording sessions with the moon as a side dish. But you see, they need a little green up front. Just to cover expenses, you see, the cost of a demo CD, the cost of mailing, a little extra money to take care of lunch and drinks or dinner with a recording rep. I don't have time for agents, Mr. Graham. I thank you for the beer."

Doc stood up. He finished his beer and set the mug on the table.

"Sit down, Doc."

"Beg pardon?"

Dexter stared into Doc's face. The smile was gone. He was two dark eyes and a black beard glaring at Doc. "Sit down. I'm not through."

Doc sat down.

"I'm not an agent." Dexter folded his hands and leaned across the table, talking underneath the country swing that played on the speakers. "You saw all that gear in my studio. I don't want any money from you. Now or in the future. All I want to do is help your career."

"Right. You drop into my life one day and out of the goodness of your heart decide to help me make the big time."

Dexter smiled again. He leaned back. "The things I do out of the goodness of my heart I do for people I know and love, Doc. I don't know you or love you, though I think a lot of your musical abilities. No. I'm doing this for money. It's how I make my living. And you'll be making money, too. Are you interested in money, Doc?"

Doc grinned. "Naw. Not me. How much? How?"

"You play the guitar and I'll take care of the rest."

A group of musicians had come in from the back and begun to set up on the stage. They all wore cowboy hats and blue jeans.

"This isn't really my scene," Doc said. "This is a cowboy bar."

38

Dexter nodded. "I know. You play jazz and blues. I've heard you. You're out of the Bill Broonzy and Muddy Waters and Sonny Terry and Brownie McGhee tradition. I've heard that you're a white Robert Johnson. You can play with a bunch of country boys in a minute. They might surprise you. These aren't hick musicians here."

Doc studied Dexter as the band began to play. The little speech on blues had surprised him. Maybe this guy knew what he was doing.

"You mean you want me to audition?" Doc said. "Is that what this is about? You need a guitarist?"

Dexter growled a gurgly chuckle. He motioned to the bartender for more drinks.

"Sandy's already paid you, Doc. This ain't no tryout. I just want you to play with the band and have a good time. No strings. Whatever you want to drink for the rest of the night is on me."

Doc had learned early in life that nothing ever comes free. Or easy, for that matter. But in his pocket were a hundred dollars wanting to be spent. He had a guitar ready to be played. There was booze waiting to be drunk and an audience starting to trickle in.

Doc grinned at Dexter. "Okay. If these guys are willing, I'll sit in."

"They're willing," Dexter said. I've already seen to that."

"I figured you had." Doc leaned back and sipped on his beer.

Dexter went to the bandstand. One of the guitar players bent over and Dexter talked into his ear. The musician looked toward Doc and nodded as he listened. Then Dexter went to the bar and talked to the bartender. He handed the bartender a bill. The musicians worked through Creedence Clearwater's "Fortunate Son." It was a standard quartet, with a lead guitar, rhythm, bass and drums. The music vibrated along the wooden dance floor. Every table was full, and the room was noisy with the music, chatter, bartenders mixing drinks, people laughing and drinking. Doc went to the side of the stage, sat down with his guitar and began quietly chording along with the band to warm up.

A voice came in his ear. "You 'bout ready to play?" The rhythm guitarist was bent over, shouting at Doc over the music. "I'm going to introduce you after this song."

39

Doc looked up. "Introduce me?"

The rhythm man had already left.

Doc stood up and strapped his guitar over his shoulder like a gunfighter buckling on his guns before stepping into the street to kill a man. He looked out at the audience.

Nobody was paying any attention to the band. The musicians brought the song to an end. Applause flickered through the room. The rhythm guitarist went to the microphone at center stage.

"We got a special treat for you tonight," he said. "An old friend has stopped by. If you've ever been to the Century Sky Room, you've already recognized him. Let's bring him up now, blues legend Doc Blevins. Here he is, the doctor of the blues."

Doc stepped up onto the stage, carrying his guitar at his side. He walked to the center of the platform and turned to face the band. The place was quiet, sort of like a small town gets when a new family moves in and everybody stops their life to study and wonder over the strangers.

"What do you boys want to play?"

"Your call, Doc," the rhythm player said.

"I'm a Man," Doc said. "That alright?"

The lead guitar player smiled. "Lemme give you an intro, Doc." He laid his guitar down and took a harmonica out of his shirt pocket. He tapped his foot four times on the wooden floor, then blew into the harmonica, a wailing progression of notes starting at A and weaving up and down the scale, settling into a swingy A-D-C.

Doc strummed back and forth from the C to the A. He looked into the crowd, found a woman in a blue denim skirt at a front table, stepped to the mike and leaned forward. He looked at the denim woman and sang in his tenor voice.

"Now when I was a little boy,

"At the age of five.

"I had somethin' in my pocket

"Keep a lot of folks alive.

"Now I'm a man.

"I spell it M,

"Aaaaaaa

40

"Nnnnnn.

"Man.

Doc drew the word out. "I'm a mayan."

He stepped back and played in and out of the melody as the drummer carried a steady bass thump thump thump thump, clapping the high hat cymbals together every second and fourth beat. The rhythm player picked up the chord progression that Doc had dropped off. The bass man, playing an electric, strode along the bottom of the piece. Doc went back to the mike.

"All you pretty women,"

He looked into the face of the denim woman.

"Stand in line.

"I can make love to ya baby.

"In a hour's time.

"I'm a mayan.

"Aw." Doc growled into the microphone, playing a lead solo line between vowels.

"Aw." He moaned, filling the room with his voice. "Awwwww."

He turned his back to the audience, looked down at his guitar and sent his fingers up and down the strings, pushing blues notes out of his guitar, through the electric wires into the amplifier and through the dance hall. He closed his eyes and played the song like it was new. When he turned around to sing again, he found the audience looking back at him. The whole room listened. A white light attached to a small black camera cut through the crowd. Somebody was recording the goddam thing. Doc grinned, looked at the rhythm player and winked.

"We got 'em," he said.

The rhythm player smiled and nodded, and the two stepped forward, playing in unison as Doc sang out the song. They brought it to a close, facing each other across the space of five feet as they strummed the blues piece dead. Whistles and whoops filled the room.

Doc looked over at the booth, where Dexter sat with his beer in front of him, his eyes intent, his hands folded beneath his chin, watching it all. He was alone. Sandy had disappeared after bringing Doc and Dexter their first drinks.

The waitress stopped in front of the bandstand and handed a glass of whiskey to Doc. He held it up to the audience, tilted his head back and swigged it down in three gulps. He smacked his lips and stepped to the mike.

"That was nice," he said, combing his hair back with the fingers of his right hand. "Here's another one."

He turned to face the band, tapped his foot fast and picked out the introductory notes to Muddy Waters' "Got My Mojo Working." The musicians picked it up. Dancers mobbed the floor.

For three sets, Doc led the band through blues and rhythm-and-blues standards. Dexter was right about the musicians. They were hot, staying with Doc, even pushing him along. Sometimes he and the band's regular lead guitar player exchanged licks. Mostly, the lead player handled the harmonica, weaving in and out of Doc's guitar as if they'd rehearsed the pieces at the Sky Room. The room was packed, as people danced and others crowded around the stage, facing the musicians, swaying their hips and bellies in time to the music. Smoke rolled out the open front door onto the parking lot, where people leaned against cars and stood on the asphalt, smoking cigarettes and taking drinks from open bottles of beer or passing joints back and forth.

Between the last two sets, Doc took a tumbler of whiskey out the back door. He leaned against the wall of the nightclub and took gulps of warm booze and fresh air. He was playing well. His fingers hit the strings true. The music was lively tonight. It was like a good night at the Sky Room, when he and Grady played so hard that they sweat and panted, and Doc went home tired. It was a good tired, and good music, and Doc slept late the next day, anxious to go out at night and be in the club and play again.

It was cool outside. The stars barely shone through the haze of city lights. Doc breathed in the air and listened to the jukebox music that pushed through the cracks of the doorway and windows. Inside, he could hear the toilets flushing, people laughing and yelling to each other, the cash register jingling. A man stumbled around the corner of the building, unzipped his pants and pissed a steaming stream of urine against the back wall. He zipped up, looked over and saw Doc watching him.

"Hey brother," he said. "Some party tonight."

"Yeah." Doc took a sip of whiskey.

The man looked down at himself. He grinned. "John's full. Waiting line." He laughed and disappeared around the corner.

At the end of the night, Doc and Dexter sat in the booth, fresh drinks in front of them. Doc's eyes were half closed. Cigarette smoke misted the room.

"What do you think of those hick musicians now?" Dexter said.

"Yeah." Doc tried to sit up straight. He stared at Dexter. "They were fine. Just fine."

"But you made the show, Doc."

Doc nodded. He was sleepy.

"Drink up, Doc. Don't worry about driving. We'll get you home."

Doc took a long drink. The room was warm. He felt dizzy.

"Doc, let's make a business deal. Let's make me your manager."

"I don't need no managers. No agents. No managers."

Dexter pulled a piece of paper out of his inside jacket pocket. He laid it on the table in front of Doc.

"Sign this, Doc. All it says is you're going to make lots of money, and I'll get part of it for managing you. It says we're going to record you, we're going to distribute the CDs and DVDs, with you getting a percentage. It says you're going to do a concert tour. I don't get any money unless you make money. Read number five. It says that right there. You have to make money before I make money."

"How much? I already got a job."

"I'll guarantee what you made tonight every single night that you play for me. The guarantee doubles – it's in the contract, just read the thing – when we reach a certain level of contract. When you go out on the road, you'll get your guarantee, plus a percentage of the house. You also get a percentage of the DVD and CD sales. That's where you really make the money. Those audience members, they get all drunk and they line up to buy the CDs and DVDs at the end of the show. It's a no-lose deal, Doc. It's what you've been working for all your life."

"A hundred dollars? For what I did tonight?"

"Plus all you can drink and living and eating expenses. And a percentage of the cover charge and sales, remember. Tonight's house is better than two grand."

Doc lifted the whiskey glass and looked through it. Dexter's head was just above the line of whiskey. "That's a lot of booze. I've had years of practice."

"I know. Sign this paper, Doc. It's only for three months, but renewable. It's got a clause that lets you out early if you want out, with certain stipulations. Look at number eleven. In three months we negotiate again if we both want to."

"I only make $300 a week at Maggio's." Doc peered into the whiskey glass again, back about twenty years. "I've been on the road before. We put together a band a few years ago and toured the country." He chuckled at the memory that came at him, a motel room where he and Will Simmons, a bass man, played poker until 4 a.m. and finally decided the final, hundred-dollar pot, with a cut of the deck while the rest of the band snored, stretched out on the couch and the two beds. The front door was open and you could hear the wind moan outside now and then.

Doc took Dexter's pen, pulled at his chin, and then signed on the black line at the bottom, right next to where Dexter's index finger was pointing.

Dexter pulled off a copy and handed it to Doc.

"Let's go, Doc," he said. "You need some sleep."

Doc stood up, grabbed his guitar case and walked behind Dexter. Cigarette butts and puddles of beer lay on the floor between the rows of tables and chairs. A small, dark man with a moustache, wearing a T-shirt and blue work pants, pushed a vacuum hose along the floor while the jukebox blared a steel guitar.

Across town, Vicki lay half asleep in the blackness of her apartment. She felt Doc as he sat on the edge of the bed. She listened to his story.

"I really had it tonight, Vick," he said.

Vicki nodded. It was a reprise of an old, worn tune, but with a new chord or two thrown in: a road trip and a contract.

"Man, you should've seen it. I didn't want to do it at first. I mean, this was a shitkicker dive, and the band was a cowboy band.

44

But this Dexter cat, he kept layin' on the booze and flashin' this money in my face. Vicki, these guys could play. I mean they could get down and play. And they were behind me. It was like it was my band. It was my show."

Vicki listened as Doc told his story, stopping now and then to gulp down a drink of whiskey.

"Doc. Did you sign the contract?"

"You bet." Doc patted his rear pocket, where he kept his wallet. "It's right here. It's a done deal."

"Oh, Doc."

"What? What?"

"I wish you would've let somebody read it first. How drunk were you?"

Doc rubbed Vicki's leg through the blanket. A cricket chirped outside the open window. Cool morning air pushed into the room. Vicki could feel Doc's smile. The bed jiggled as he talked.

"It's fine Vicki. Three months, that's all, and then I'll have a stake to put together my own band, find my own club, set up a deal like Grady's."

"But Grady's invited you into his gig."

Doc shook his head. "I don't care. I mean, I like Grady, you know that. But it's still his club, his gig. I want my own. Besides. Who knows where this thing might lead? I couldn't let this deal go, Vick."

"I know." Vicki smiled in the darkness. She did know. She knew this was coming. Her friends had warned her against a musician. Her instinct had cautioned her. She lay her head back on the pillow.

She knew that some day this musician she'd stumbled onto would go away. Maybe he would be back, maybe not. She knew Doc had to try this, she knew Doc had to move on. She knew the blues was more than a song. She knew the blues was real life.

She listened as Doc left the bedroom and went down the hall. The front room lamp flicked on, and then the stereo. Jazz guitar chords wafted into the room. A moon with misty rings around it shone into the bedroom window and made pale ghosts dance on the hardwood floor.

She sat up again. A breeze brushed against her damp forehead. The smell of whiskey lingered. Vicki got out of bed and went into the living room. Doc snored softly on the couch. She turned the stereo off and looked at the digital numbers that glowed red on the tuner's clock. It was 4:30 in the morning.

She put a pot of water on the stove in the kitchen. She moved in the darkness like a blind woman, taking a mug from the cabinets, a saucer, the jar of instant coffee.

Everything was in its place in her apartment. Vicki had lived there for five years before Doc came. She would be there long after he left. He was a brief interlude in her life, coming into it like a song interrupts a quiet afternoon with a certain tune or phrase that strikes you, stays with you for awhile, then drifts on into the memory.

Vicki returned to the living room, the coffee cup steaming into the air. She sank into the easy chair next to the couch, set her cup on the end table and watched Doc sleep.

Doc stood at Dexter's doorway and looked up at a blue, midmorning sky as he knocked. He heard guitar music behind the door. It sounded just like the band from the club last night.

Dexter opened the door. "C'mon in here, Doc. I want to show you something."

Doc stepped into the living room studio. The smell of coffee filled the room. Dexter shoved the door shut with his foot.

"Look at that." Dexter pointed to the television screen.

Doc was on TV, playing his guitar. Behind him was the band from the night before. The camera zoomed in for a closeup of Doc's face as Doc began singing a tune.

"I put a spell on you," Doc's lips mouthed closeup, as his guitar tremeloed in the background.

"Yeah, I ain't gonna take none of your foolin' around.

"I ain't gonna take none of your puttin' me down.

"I put a spell on you.

"Because you're mine."

A squealing guitar blues riff came in as the camera zoomed to Doc's fingers on the strings.

Doc grinned at himself.

"Looks pretty good," he said. "I wondered who that was with the camera last night."

"There's a whole bunch you don't know and that you don't have to worry about."

Doc looked at Dexter. He wore a solid black necktie over a pressed blue shirt, gray slacks, shiny black loafers. His hair was parted neatly and combed back. The earring was gone.

"You look pretty good," Dexter said. "You look like a blues guy. Except for one thing."

"Yeah?"

"You need some whiskers. The eyes are fine. They're bloodshot. Your hair has some gray in it." He looked at Doc and flashed a grin. "You've been around some. But you'd look better with some stubble."

"I shave every day."

Dexter was watching the monitor again. He punched a button and the screen went blank. The only sound was the soft whir of the tape rewinding.

"Mind you, this'll work," he said. "Your face had a good shadow on it last night. And we want different shots of you so it's clear there's a passage of time on this thing. But tonight I want you unshaven."

"Tonight?"

"I got a gig set up at a club on the east side. You may know it. Billy's?"

"Biker bar," Doc said.

"Yeah. Anyway, they've got a blues jam tonight. I've called a few musicians. I've made all the arrangements. It'll be your jam. Now watch this."

"I could go for some of that coffee."

"Help yourself. It's in the kitchen."

When Doc came back, Dexter started the recording from the beginning. It showed the rhythm guitarist introducing Doc, just like happened the night before, but the next shot was of the crowd, standing and hollering and clapping. Then the camera went back to the stage and showed Doc playing Willie Dixon's "Gonna Bring It On Home." He hadn't played that song until nearly the end of the night. The camera moved in on the bass player, then panned to Doc, who was grinning at the bassist.

"That isn't how it happened," Doc said.

Dexter gave a look like Doc had just landed from outer space.

"It is now," Dexter said. He left the recording running, turned down the volume and went to the computer across the room. He typed in some commands. A printer at the end of the desk spewed out a piece of white paper. Dexter ripped the paper off the machine.

Doc fiddled with some knobs, trying to restore some volume to the recording. He watched himself strum the guitar and mouth a song as he turned a dial.

Then Dexter's hands were on his, jerking them away from the tuning and volume buttons. Dexter pushed Doc halfway across the room.

"Don't ever touch my gear." Dexter stared into Doc's face, his cheeks red, his eyes wide open, intent on Doc. "Ever. I don't touch your guitar, do I? You think of this gear as my guitar, got it?"

Doc lifted his hands in surrender. "Sorry, man. I just thought, I thought ..."

"Don't think. That's my job. You just play. I'll take care of the rest."

Then, like a wave passed over him, Dexter relaxed his face. The red was gone. He smiled like Doc was an old, trusted friend.

"Here. Look at this." Dexter handed one of the computer printouts to Doc.

"Sheet music? I don't read." Doc smiled. "It's a joke. These are just numbers and letters to me. That's all."

"Yeah, they're numbers," Dexter said. "Study them. They're interesting numbers."

Doc scanned the printout and rows of characters.

"Look at number one," Dexter said. "See the number to the right of it? Forty-nine percent?"

Doc nodded.

"That's the number of adult females between the ages of 25 and 40 who listen to blues at least once a week."

Doc nodded. "Okay."

"Look at the number in the same location on the next line. What is it?"

"Thirty-five percent."

"Right. That's the same age group and sex, only for country music."

"Okay."

"That's not the norm. At least, it hasn't been for the past several months.Country has beaten blues consistently. Until now."

"Until now?"

"Until this sampling, which was taken five weeks ago."

Doc scratched his head. "What's it mean?"

"We're in a blip. I don't know how long it'll last, what causes it or how it got here. That's for the sociologists. But the numbers don't lie, my guitar-playing friend. Believe me, this research is accurate. People with buying power, disposable income, they're listening to your kind of music. They're digging blues right now. A good number of them are going to the clubs with blues bookings."

Dexter was smiling at him, holding the printout in the air.

"What, you get off on numbers?" Doc said.

"These numbers tell me what the market is out there. I deal in music, Doc. I'm a consultant to radio stations, to nightclub owners. I own some clubs. I manage a few bands. But more than that, I'm a marketer, and music is what I market. I sell music, Doc. You play music, I sell it like supermarkets sell sausage. These computer printouts are like my weather report if I'm a farmer. Or my stock market listing if I'm a broker on Wall Street. Get it? They tell me that right now, people are into the blues. Call it a low-pressure system that's moved into the area, and I think it's here to stay for a while. I think people are tired of big arena concerts, they're tired of all the country players singin' the same old bullshit – and that's only a marketing judgment, Doc, I happen to be a country fan myself." Dexter showed his teeth in a quick grin. "Basically, Doc, I think your time has come."

"Oh, yeah?" Doc pulled on his chin. "Well that's good."

"Yeah. That's good." Dexter went back to the computer and sat down. He stared into the screen and punched commands into the keyboard, playing it fast 'and easy like a jazz pianist strolling through a boogie woogie. Doc finished off his coffee and went to the door.

"Going out?" Dexter looked up from the desk.

"I'm going to find some breakfast."

"There's a diner one block over. Go down to the sidewalk, then to your left, then to your left again."

Doc went outside. The apartment was in an older district of town where residential neighborhoods were beginning to transition into warehouses. The tops of the city's tallest buildings were visible from the front porch. He went down the metal steps and followed Dexter's directions to the café, which was on a two-lane thoroughfare. He passed a drug store and thrift shop before finding the café, a small, brick storefront with a row of stools along a green counter. Three small tables, each with four chairs, were pushed against the wall opposite the counter.

A man in a greasy, green baseball cap and blue work shirt with the sleeves rolled up sat a couple of stools away from the door. Grease smudged his arms. Black gook lined his fingernails. He swabbed egg yolk with a piece of toast and took a bite. He looked up and nodded at Doc. Two stools down, another man stared straight ahead, his hand wrapped around a coffee mug. A small table radio on a chopping block table next to the refrigerator broadcast an acoustic guitar strumming a folksy cowboy tune while a female voice bemoaned a crying night at home.

A woman in a white uniform and red, checkered apron came from the back. She set a brown cup in front of Doc and filled it with hot coffee.

"You know what you want yet, hon?"

Doc grinned. He wanted to take this diner home with him and put it in a song. He wanted to play a guitar tune that these people would like. He wanted to take diners like this one and freeze them in time so there would always be places like this despite the plant-filled, brass-railed chain restaurants filling up the country. "I'd like two eggs over medium, a side of hash browns, a couple sticks of bacon and some toast."

"White or wheat bread?"

"Wheat."

She turned around, took a couple of eggs from the refrigerator and cracked them onto the black grill behind the counter. She dropped two pieces of bread into the toaster, then she grabbed the glass coffee pot and filled a few cups up and down the counter.

Doc listened to the place. A low voice on the radio said a warm weather front was moving into the city that night, and then he introduced another song. The waitress rubbed the counter with a damp cloth. She stopped in front of the man on the stool downstream from Doc's.

"Where'd you end up last night?" She picked up his cup and wiped under it. Blue eyeshadow weighed down her eyelids, and her eyebrows were a glossy black. Her hair was mostly blonde, except for the half inch of black growing out of the scalp.

"We went to Hank's and had a few beers. Then Jim and Myrna got into one of their scuffles."

"Jesus Mae, what about this time? As though it mattered what those two fight about."

"Same ol' same ol'. She wants him to get a job, he wants to wait until the right thing comes along, and then she started threatening to kick him out again."

Doc's last conversation with Vicki came at him in bits and pieces, starting with his explanation about hooking up with Dexter and Sandy. At first, Vicki thought this whole thing was about Sandy. She thought Doc had found someone new, and the other stuff, the road tour and contract, was a side bit to the main story: Doc and Sandy.

"If you got a fault, Vick, it's your goddam insecurity and jealousy."

"C'mon, Doc, get real. You feed me some story about strangers coming along and whisking you away with promises of concert tours and never-never land. Why don't you just tell me you met some goddam woman at the club and went home with her? Why all the deception?"

And then, the same old soothing line from Doc. "C'mon, Vick. I'm not your ex-old man. This is Doc here. Doc who digs you. You'd know if I was tired of you. This has nothing to do with another woman. It has something to do with every musician's dream, even if it is happening in a funny way."

Vicki sighed. "Yeah. I know. You're right. But you got to admit, Doc, it's a pretty fantastic story."

Doc shook his head. People put so much work and time into finding someone, then once they do, half their effort is put into fighting and worrying and doing everything but enjoying the thing they were looking for.

"Everything all right, hon?" The waitress poured fresh coffee into Doc's cup.

"Just fine."

She smiled and walked away. The first man, with the dirty fingernails, was gone. Now it was just the three of them and the music on the radio. Doc wondered if the waitress and her customers were the sort of people Dexter was going after when he was working up his printouts.

No. These diner people have their music priorities set, and it's just a soundtrack to their lives. They listen to the music that fits their drink and their mood, and sometimes they find someone to get up and dance to it with them. These people don't buy the blues, but there wouldn't be any blues without them. Doc took a twenty dollar bill from his wallet and gave it to the waitress. She smiled at him as she counted out his change. She had a gold tooth in her smile. Doc laid a dollar bill on the counter and put the rest of the bills in with the four twenties he had left.

It felt good to have more than $80 in his wallet and a belly full of food.

Doc found Sandy sitting in the swivel office chair of the computer desk when he returned. She wore a tight pair of cords, cowboy boots, a red and white checkered shirt and a bourbon and cola in her right hand. Dexter was gone.

"Have a good breakfast?"

Doc passed a toothpick from the left to the right side of his mouth. "Pretty hard to mess up bacon and eggs."

"That diner does a good job. Try their cheeseburger sometime. It'll stop up your blood vessels for a day." She smiled, swirled her drink a couple of times so the ice cubes clinked against the glass, and she took a long sip.

"Just what is it you do around here?" Doc went to the refrigerator and found a beer.

"My job title is administrative assistant."

Doc nodded.

"Right now, my assignment is you. Dexter has a lot of projects going on. He owns the club you were at last night. He has a production company. He does stuff I don't even know about. And he's good at it. All legit far as I know. Everything I've seen him touch comes up green. As in money."

"Okay. I'm sold. But you still haven't told me. Just what is it that you do?"

"My Friday night job description is to drive around town in the wee hours of the morning and pick up lonely guitar players standing in front of pawn shops. Later I take them to buy new clothes."

"I don't need new clothes today." Doc smiled. She was quick.

"How about some old clothes?"

"Those I already got."

Sandy stood up. "Seriously, Doc. Today my orders are to take you clothes shopping. Consider it part of your new job."

Doc swallowed a couple of gulps of beer. "Then maybe you can tell me just what it is I do around here."

"You play the guitar."

"That. And grow whiskers. And wear new clothes."

"Now practice working that job description into a resume." Sandy emptied her drink and took the glass of stranded ice cubes to the kitchen. She grabbed her jean jacket from the back of the chair and walked to the door. "But there'll be more. Trust me. Your official job title, I'm authorized to announce, is famous blues musician."

Doc guzzled the last of the beer and took another can for the road. They stood at the top of the porch for a minute, looking toward the city. The sun hung in the middle of the blue ceiling. The air above the city was a mixture of brown and gray. A squirrel clung to the side of an elm tree between the studio and the street.

Doc slid open the door of the van's passenger side. Sandy drove toward the city. He leaned his head back and watched out the window as the trees and houses and stores slid by. People walked along the sidewalk, or gathered in pairs in front of a chain link fence to talk about how hot the summer would be, whether there might be an autumn this year, or maybe summer would just bump right into winter like it did last year, without any fall. As Sandy drove into town, Doc closed his eyes and remembered clothes buying from years ago. His father had gone away, searching for a piano job or a new family or a quiet drink – whatever it is that fathers abandoning their wives and children are looking for. Doc and his mother had moved to an upstairs apartment downtown. His mother was driving him to buy new clothes for school. It was a warm day, just like this, but cold at night, the edge of change in seasons and in life.

His mother had taken a job as a secretary in a real estate office. The job required her to dress nicely on a small salary.

She shopped well. They went to the department stores downtown, downstairs to the bargain basements, where seconds with badly sewn buttons and mis-seamed collars went for 30 to 40 percent off.

"And nobody but you knows there's anything wrong," she said.

And she was right. His clothes looked just like anyone else's, though the brand was not the same as the other kids'. And nobody knew the difference.

Except him.

"We're here," Sandy said.

"Where?"

"The downtown Goodwill."

Doc looked at her. "I thought you said new clothes."

"Actually, I said old. But they were new once, and some of them are good as new."

Doc smiled. "Were you ever a mother?"

"Not yet." She slid her door open. "I guess I've been lucky so far."

They went into the Goodwill.

"Have a ball," Sandy said. "Dexter says you should look bluesy. Whatever that means."

Doc studied the rows of used clothing, shoes stacked in shelves, suits on hangers, shirts folded on tables. "I haven't had this much fun since I was a kid shopping for school clothes," Doc said. He saw a sport coat he liked and headed for the coat rack and began his shopping spree.

That night, Doc Blevins, would-be famous blues musician, wore the seedlings of a beard, a used pair of baggy gray slacks, a white button-down shirt rolled up to the elbows and covered with an unbuttoned Navy blue sweater vest, and he invaded a biker bar on the east side of town, where he sat in with the blues house band. He took center stage, he chuckled and grinned along with the other musicians, he swallowed glasses of whiskey and chased them with cold beers, he squeezed the neck of his guitar and wrung fresh blues out of it.

Men in blue jeans and sunglasses and black and gray beards stopped their pool games and stood, leaning on their pool cues, to watch Doc play. They pulled tattooed women to the small tile dance floor in front of the stage and they did the biker version of the Shitkicker Shuffle:

Now put your left foot in, left foot out, right foot in, right foot out, clasp your hands behind your back, now shake that flabby belly all about.

Through it all, a man with a video recorder moved among the tables and bar, panning the crowd, zooming in on Doc's grizzled face, his lips set tightly as he pressed bar chords and plucked leads. The recorder whirred quietly beneath the rumble of music in the small beer and whiskey bar.

Sandy sat at the bar and watched it all, swallowing an assembly-line procession of drinks until closing time, when she drove Doc home and left him at the front door with instructions on what to wear and what time to be ready the next day.

She and Doc repeated the scene for the next couple of weeks, as Doc sat in with country bands, blues bands, rock bands and even a jazz combo, spending his days in bed, drinking afternoon beers in the city parks while Dexter and Sandy recorded and edited and dubbed and redubbed in the small studio on the other side of town.

Then, one summer night, as the dew was beginning to gather on the grass in the yard, Vicki fell asleep on the couch in her living room. One lamp was on, throwing a dim spotlight on an orange tabby cat that sat on its haunches on the arm of the couch, licking its paw. The 11 o'clock news had just ended. Vicki snored softly through the commercial zone that separates prime time from zombie time, the lonely part of the night when the only thing keeping people from their desperation and fears is an old gray-and-white '50s movie television with a warped sound track on the TCM channel.

A picture of Doc playing his guitar came on the TV screen. "James Doctor Blevins," said a deep voice as the television zoomed in on Doc's face, his eyes squinting as he worked his fingers up and down the guitar frets. "Legendary roadhouse blues veteran coming your way on DVD." The camera moved back and the titles of songs began to roll over the screen. "Spoonful."

56

"Hootchie Coochie." "Kansas City." "Good Morning School Girl."

"In the tradition of Muddy Waters, Howlin' Wolf, Sonny Boy Williamson, the blues doctor himself plays the blues standards on Roadway Blues, a compilation of a blues career that's spanned nearly four decades, following the Mississippi River north from New Orleans to Chicago and to nightclubs across the country."

The camera slowly panned across a packed, smoky nightclub. It showed people dancing, standing and applauding, hollering, as the titles of more songs appeared. "Key to the Highway." "Gypsy Woman."

Doc came back on the screen, holding a glass of booze in his hand, his red guitar hanging from his neck. He grinned broadly through a gray shadow of whiskers as he watched a harmonica player blow a plaintive shriek. "Roadway Blues, a phenomenal collection from the blues master they call Doctor Blues, is available now on DVD for $19.95," the voice said as Doc leaned over and coaxed a boogie shuffle from his guitar. "Also available on CD. Call now. That's Roadhouse Blues." A phone number and mailing address appeared on the screen as the camera slowly moved back from the stage. Doc strummed and sang a slow "Bring It On Home" while a harmonica whispered behind him.

"I think about the way you love me too.

"You can bet your life I'm comin' home to you.

"Gonna bring it on home now.

"Bring it on home to you."

And later that night after Vicki had moved her sleep into the bedroom, Doc came quietly into the apartment and gathered a few clothes, his acoustic guitar. He carried them outside to the van, where Sandy was waiting with the engine running.

Doc stood over Vicki in the bedroom, then he bent over and kissed her. She opened her eyes.

"I'm going now."

"Where?"

"On the road. The concert gig. I told you."

"Oh. Yeah. I guess I fell asleep. You get your stuff?"

"Yeah. I didn't want to wake you. But I wanted to say goodbye."

"You were supposed to be home earlier tonight. I made a dinner for us." Vicki sat up. "Now? You're leaving now?"

"Yeah. First show is in a couple of days."

"Where?"

"College town. Laramie, Wyoming."

"That's no college town. That's shitsville."

They laughed, then talked quietly in the dark bedroom. Doc could hear the engine of the van going out in the alley. Then he kissed Vicki again and was gone.

Sandy backed the van out of the gravel parking spot behind the house and into the alley. Vicki's tomato patch grew a few feet from the van. Doc remembered the Sunday he and Vicki had planted the seedlings. That night they sat on folding lawn chairs next to the garden, drinking beers and watching the young plants, and Vicki talked about the gardens her father had grown when she was a girl.

"I guess this is the closest I've got to home," Doc said to Sandy. "At least, it has been for the last couple of years. God, is that all I've known her? Just a couple of years?"

Sandy handed him the whiskey bottle. They drove down the dark alley and into the deserted street. Doc looked up at the streetlight on the corner, a teardrop of white light hanging down from the thin, black pole. He swished a mouthful of whiskey from cheek to cheek and rolled down the window. The breeze came in and blew across his forehead as the van's headlights groped into the night.

Big, heavy raindrops slammed onto the windshield and burst into splats of water. The steady tic-toc of the windshield wiper took them away, clearing the glass for a moment. Outside Doc's window, blurry green fields zipped by. Cool air pushed through the small crack of the window.

The radio played twangy country blues that melted into another song and then another, with nasal voices honking and wailing above the guitars and snare drums.

Doc leaned back in the passenger seat and closed his eyes as Sandy drove them between towns. He let his mind drift backward to Ike Mann.

He used to sit in the back booth of The Palmer House restaurant, where the swinging wooden doors separated the men and their whiskey from the families and their fried chicken and mashed potato dinners.

Doc ordered Cokes and leaned into the aisle, peering through the slats of the doors as Ike played the blues, backed by a harmonica man, a pianist, a bass player and a drummer.

One time he pushed through the door and stood in Ike's dark blues world, with the shining liquor glasses standing in rows behind the bar, the men and women on the stools along the side of the bar with their cigarettes glowing and glasses of booze in front of them, talking about secret sins while Ike sat on the small stage, his black face framed by a neatly trimmed white beard. Ike rocked back and forth, stomping his right foot on the floor as his fingers went over the strings.

It was like each finger had its own brain, its own life independent of the other fingers. They went off in four different directions while the right hand picked and strummed the strings.

A harsh whisper blew into the boy's ear. "You know you don't belong here, Jimmy."

He looked up. One of the barmaids, with a tray of empty glasses, stood next to him.

"Git back into the restaurant. You want us to lose our license?"

"How old is he, Edith?" the boy said as he backed out of the bar.

"Ike? Shit, kid. He's 70 if he's a day. He's been around forever."

"Has he always played this good?"

She shook her head. "Nope. He used to play better." She stood still for a minute, balancing the tray of glasses on her upturned hand as she gazed at a memory. "Oh, he could play. I remember, we used to hang around after our shift. You couldn't help but dance when Ike played." She smiled. Then she remembered the boy. "Now get out of here."

He went back to the restaurant booth and listened to Ike's blues, the rumble of the bass, the chink-a-chink of the high-hat cymbals. Ike moaned as he sang a blues.

Outside, a big, wet snow blew against the restaurant's glass front and burst into streams of water that ran in long, clear lines down the glass. Car headlights pierced the storm and veered away. Men walked by the window, their coats wrapped around them tightly, scarves twirled around their necks. Puffs of steam came out of their nostrils.

Man, the boy thought. How can anybody play better than Ike was playing right this minute? How could anybody ever hope to play that well?

In the summertime, he sometimes was there when the bar closed. The restaurant stayed open about an hour after the bar, serving late dinners and coffee to the bar patrons. Ike told stories.

"The most amazing guitar player I ever saw," he said once, "was a man who had only a thumb and his first finger on his left hand. The rest got chopped off by a train wheel when he was a kid." The barmaids and a couple of band members were gathered at the end of the restaurant, right next to the bar. The boy sat in his booth and listened. "This guy, using that thumb and that finger, played a slide blues like I never heard in my life, all with bar chords using the first three or four strings. He had a way of bendin' that finger so's he could go up a fret and catch a couple strings on it. But the main thing was his singing. He used his voice to play some of the notes his hands couldn't. I still don't know

60

how he did it. This was when I was a boy, just learning to play."
Ike smiled.

"After he was through, he'd put his guitar down. It was a scratched up old thing. And then he'd hold up his finger and smell it like it was a hot chicken drumstick, like it smelled good enough to eat, and he'd look at us and say, 'boys, you wouldn't believe me if I told you where this finger's been. It's a wonder it isn't too worn out to play today.' And we'd all laugh. Every time we'd laugh." Ike chuckled and took his silver flask out of his old sport coat. He unscrewed the top, poured a shot of whiskey into his coffee, took a drink straight from the flask and then pocketed it.

The boy stayed until closing. As the lights of the restaurant flicked off, Ike emerged from the front door. The boy tailed him through downtown and into the residential fringe of the city's north side. He stayed back in a clump of bushes and watched Ike climb the wooden steps to his porch.

Just before going in the door, the old man turned toward the kid in the bushes. "You be careful going home, son," he said. Then he stepped into his home, where a yellow light shone behind a white curtain.

One afternoon, Doc sat with his guitar on a bench in a downtown park on Ike's homeward route. He was trying to work out a chord when a voice came from the sidewalk a few feet away.

"What're you trying to play?"

The boy looked up. "An augmented F. From an F seven."

Ike came over to the bench and sat down. "May I see your guitar?"

It was like Joe DiMaggio asking to see your baseball glove. Doc handed it over.

Ike strummed a few chords. "You know, any chord you can play on this guitar, there's at least two or three other ways to play it."

The boy nodded.

"And there are ways to cheat too. Ways that nobody'll know because it won't sound any different. Now watch this." The old guitar player made an F-7 bar chord on the first fret. Then he brought his middle two fingers down to the B and G strings and covered them on the second fret. "There," he said to the boy, "is the chord you want."

"What about the D string?"

"Don't even worry about that one if you're in a hurry. And you looked in a hurry to me."

Ike handed the instrument back. "That's a nice guitar."

"Thanks."

"Where'd you get it?"

"My father."

"He must've been a musician."

"He played the piano."

"What was his name?"

The boy smiled. "You wouldn't know him. He just messed around. A few bars maybe. Mostly dives. You know."

Ike grinned and nodded. "Don't I know you from somewhere?"

"I've been down at The Palmer House a few times. Only I'm not old enough to get into the bar."

"Yeah. I've seen you out in the restaurant. A few times. What's the deal, you like to eat a lot?"

He shook his head. "No."

"What're you doin' in there?"

"Listening to you."

The old man pulled at his chin. He looked up at the sky, at the trees with their new spring leaves.

"You wanna be a guitar player. Is that it?"

The boy nodded.

"You go to school?"

"Yes."

"How old are you?"

"Sixteen."

"Play something for me."

The boy grinned. "Here? Now?"

"Yeah."

Suddenly his fingers were bananas. He made an F bar chord that didn't play. He quickly did an A chord blues progression, then laid the guitar on his lap. "I can't do much right now."

"That's alright. I was listening when you didn't know it." He stood up. "You'll do okay. You're already doin' what you have to."

"What do you mean?"

"You're practicing. And you're listening to one of the best players around every chance you get." The old man smiled and chuckled. "The rest will come."

It was about two more weeks before Ike came out of the bar during a break and sat down with the boy in the end booth and asked him if he still wanted to be a guitar player.

"Yes," the boy said.

"Good." Ike took a napkin from the table and a pencil from his pocket and wrote down an address. He handed it to the boy.

"What's your name?"

"James. James Blevins."

"I knew a man named Blevins once. He was a doctor. Used to come into a club I played, had a different woman with him each time. And they weren't no nurses." Ike smiled. "You come to that address on a Monday afternoon. Bring your guitar."

"Really?"

The old man winked. "You c'mon by. And don't hand that address around town. That's where I live. See you later, Doc."

Ike got up and went back to the bar. The boy craned his neck around the corner and watched the old man sit down on a wooden chair among the gleaming cymbal stands, instruments and paraphernalia of the bandstand. That was what he wanted. A bandstand in a club, to play music, with people dancing, in a place where people go to feel good.

The raindrops flew wildly at the windshield. The wipers rubbed them away in a rhythmic beat-beat. Doc slapped his hands on his knee in time to the wipers, drumming out a shuffle. Sandy peered straight ahead. Beyond her, out the window, water stood in puddles surrounded by mud and patches of grass.

"I need a drink," Sandy said.

"How far are we?"

"About 30 miles. Thirty miles out here is forever."

Doc stared out the window. In the distance, the outline of a farmhouse stood barely etched into the dripping grayness. A battered blue pickup truck sat in the driveway next to the house. A feather of gray smoke was stuck in the chimney.

They got into Denver at about 3 in the afternoon. Doc's show was at 8 that night. Soundcheck with the musicians was at 6:30.

Sandy stopped at a liquor store on the outskirts of town.

"Be right back," she said. "Need anything?"

"I'll take a fifth."

The rain ran in sheets down the windshield. Cars splashed through the puddles in the street. Sandy ran out of the liquor store clutching a paper bag. She threw open the door and jumped in, bringing a gust of wetness with her.

"Sheeit, it's wet out there." She laughed and handed the booze to Doc. They sat in the van with their bottles of whiskey and listened to the rain.

"What a drag. I hate goddam stormy days." Sandy clicked on the radio and moved the tuning dial up and down the FM band until she found some country music.

"Sorry, Doc. I'm afraid I don't fall into Dexter's demography. I mean, I like your playin' and everything. But when it's shitty outside and I'm in a strange town drinking booze out of the bottle, I need my cowboy music."

Doc nodded. "They're called demographics. That's fine. I like it myself sometimes."

"You do?"

He nodded. "Western music is okay. I've played with a good steel man. It all comes from the same place." He pointed to his heart and smiled.

Sandy lifted her bottle to him, then swigged down a shot of whiskey. They drove through town. Water ran in rivers through the gutters, until it was swallowed up by drains at the end of each block. They pulled into a Budget Inn. Sandy went to the desk to check in. She took care of all the business while Doc unloaded their things from the van. A half hour later they were moved in.

"Meet me at the van at 6, okay?" Sandy said outside her room. Doc's was next door.

"If I'm not there, call me," Doc said. "I might fall asleep.

Sandy smiled. "You just slept across half of Colorado."

"I know. See you in a couple hours."

Doc stood in the empty room. He laid the guitar case on the suitcase rack and stood his acoustic in its case against the wall next to the television. He opened his two suitcases and arranged them next to each other on the second bed. A muffled guitar wailed through the wall. Sandy had found her radio station. He unwrapped a water glass at the bathroom sink and filled it halfway with whiskey, swirled the brown juice in the glass a couple of times and tossed it down his throat. The warmth crept through his body. Doc lay down on his bed, his shoes still on, and he pulled a blanket over himself.

The rain slowed to a drizzle and tapped against the window as Doc fell into a nap.

A couple of hours later the phone rang, piercing the quiet darkness of the room like an alarm clock. It was time to go to work.

They were booked for one night in the Caravan, a country/western show bar on the west side of town. Backstage, Doc munched a tuna salad sandwich and a bag of potato chips while stage hands did sound and light checks. The audience was beginning to trickle into the club, a converted warehouse with tile on the floor and row after row of tables. At the far end of the room, pinball machines and pool tables shared space with a bar; the far wall sparkled with tiers of liquor bottles and the popping red and yellow lights of the game machines. There was a small wooden dance floor like a front porch welcome mat at the front of the stage. Doc had counted the seats earlier, while he and the house band rehearsed. About two thousand. At $15 a pop. Rehearsal had gone well. Local bands were hired for backup in each town. No fancy stuff. All they had to do was play 12-bar routines behind Doc, or simple shuffles, and then get out of the way while Doc handled the lead work and the vocals.

"They'll pick up a few hundred bucks, get their name in the paper and the club owner'll frame the article and tack it up behind the bar and show it to everybody who comes through the front door for the next year," Sandy said.

A coven of groupies gathered to the side of the stage, giggling at the musicians, dropping the players' names to each other, winking at the stage hands and anybody carrying an instrument or drumstick. They sipped from glasses as they waited for Doc's traveling blues show to begin.

Doc looked across the club from behind the stage. The place swarmed with cowboy hats and blue jeans. Dexter's research was right. People were in a mood for this kind of music. Doc's show had sold out college town nightclubs and city show bars throughout the Northern Rockies the past few weeks.

He sat down next to Sandy and ran his fingers up and down the frets of the guitar. She poured fresh whiskey into her glass.

"You always seem nervous before a show," she said.

"I'm just warming up my fingers. Just like before I used to play at the club."

"No different?"

Doc laughed. "Sure. It's different. Bigger crowds. And they're all strangers. At home, I can usually pick out someone I know and play to them. And I always know the other musicians at the Sky Room. Here, I focus in on some stranger and try to imagine they're diggin' what I'm playin'.

At the club, man you'll get some drunk comin' in and he'll get up and dance along with the music with his shirt unbuttoned and a bottle of beer in his hand and a cigarette hangin' out of his mouth. And you expect it. Usually it's the same guy, someone you know, and you know that maybe he just had a fight with his old lady and he needs to cut loose. So you even play a special song for him, something you know he'll like."

"I've seen people get pretty crazy at these shows," Sandy said.

"Yeah. I know. But it's more controlled. I mean, they might throw the guy out. And that's not bad. He might be a genuine loony, for all I know. He might pull out a gun and start shooting or something. I guess that's the difference. I'm playin' for a room full of strangers now. There's no intimacy. Understand?"

"I think so. Yeah." She smiled. "You miss the club."

"A little bit. Maybe I'm getting old." He shook his head. "I miss some of it. Not the money, though. I like the pocket money now."

"Let's start with the train set tonight," Sandy said.

They had two basic sets. One was heavy on road songs and ended with Junior Parker's "Mystery Train." The other was the love set, which ended with a ballad. Sandy never decided which set to open with until she saw the crowd. Tonight's was mostly cowboys.

"One of these nights I'll fool you and throw in some new stuff. Or maybe I'll mix up the two sets." Doc winked.

Sandy held her drink on her lap and looked Doc in the face. "No you won't. Don't even kid about that, Doc. I'm calling the music. You dig? Dexter has it all figured out, scientific, how the sets help sell the CDs and DVDs."

Doc held his hands up. "Okay, okay. I know. Dex explained once. I'm the disc jockey, he's the program director. You name the tunes, I play 'em."

Doc strapped on his guitar.

A DJ from one of the city's country/western stations was at the microphone. He wore a thin, white Stetson, a neatly trimmed black beard, a satiny pink shirt and stiff blue jeans that could have been ironed onto his legs. His shiny black and silver cowboy boots had never stepped within five feet of cow shit.

"Ladies and gentlemen. That doesn't include you, Roy." The DJ looked down and smirked at a big man with a black ten-gallon cowboy hat and a thin beard smudged across his red, fat cheeks. Laughter sprinkled the front section. "It's my pleasure to bring on stage a man you've all heard of. At least, you should have, if you've been listening to the right radio station the past few days."

A few whoops circled the room.

"This guy's played with the best, he's been puttin' out for a good four decades now and he's still going strong. Stronger than ever. But you youngsters out there won't appreciate the meaning of that."

A shout came from the back rows. "Yo! Momma! Ow!" The DJ chuckled into the microphone. "But seriously, folks. I wanna bring on a living blues legend. If you've been listening to the station, you already know what I'm talking about. If you haven't, you're about to find out. So sit back, here's the cure for what ails ya, backed by Denver's own Trail Ridge Outlaws, Doctor Blues Blevins!"

Applause and whistles rang through the room. Doc wandered onto the stage wearing threadbare brown, cuffed slacks, blue work shirt and brown sweater vest. He nodded to the band, thumped his foot on the stage floor four times and jumped into John Lee Hooker's "Boom Boom."

For an hour and a half, Doc worked methodically through the playlist of the train set, starting the crowd out with a couple of rockers, moving into the slower tunes, including some acoustical guitar strumming blues, then slowly building the audience back up with electric stuff. He played it by rote, almost like he was working scales, following Sandy's format as the tunes had appeared in his video.

"That's what the concert crowd wants, Doc," she had said as they drove between towns early on the tour. "They want to see you play, but they want to hear the songs like they're on the discs."

"Why don't they just stay home and get high and listen to the music there? I'm used to improvising on stage."

"Doc." She sipped from the booze that was always with her, usually in a covered plastic coffee mug. "I'm not a pop psychologist. I guess they like to tell their friends they saw you play. Maybe they want to see if you really can play like you do on the disc."

She sighed. "Maybe they just like to hear it like it is when they party at home. I don't know."

Doc gazed out onto the scene of heads bobbing with the music, the tables full of glasses that reflected the colored lights of the place, the glint of eyeglasses like a thousand tiny campfires, the solo men and women dancing by themselves next to the tables, clapping their hands to the music as they stared up at Doc and the band.

They yelped when he bent the strings from one note to the next. They responded with Yes! and Amen! when he filled an interval with a be-bop run of notes. By the end of the show just after 11 or so, they all were on their feet, stomping, dancing, grinning, reeling and bouncing with the music. Doc bent over his guitar, stepped to the edge of the stage and gritted his teeth as he grimaced and yanked yet another lead run out of the electric strings, as he strummed one more series of chords, until he stood, sweating, in front of the crowd that was clapping and shouting for another song.

It always ended after two sets with the sudden flash of light that brought the show to an abrupt end, people caught in mid clap, the boozers rushing to throw down the last of their liquor, dried splotches of spilled beer on the floor, doormen moving steadily among the audience members, pointing them toward the doors, where the night air sucked the noise and the stench of alcohol out of the room.

Sandy worked the table selling CDs and DVDs. The line was already about twenty drunks long as Doc went backstage and shook hands with the other musicians. Dexter had told him this was where some of the real money was made. The rhythm guitarist wiped his strings with a rag and laid his instrument in his case. "I'm goin' to another club," he told Doc. "I'm gonna jam some. Wanna come?"

Doc smiled and shook his head. "I'm tired, son. But thanks."

"Sure thing. Nice show."

Doc nodded. The drummer said he was going home to prop himself in front of the TV with a six-pack and his old lady. The house band's lead guitarist invited Doc into a poker game at his place.

No. Thanks. Doc sat in a folding metal chair and sipped from the glass of whiskey Sandy handed him. He watched the technicians close the stage down, then he stepped outside and finished off his drink under the glare of a spotlight that shone on a nearly empty asphalt parking lot. In the distance, a cricket chirped.

At the motel, Doc showered off the sweat and smell of the concert hall. He opened the door of his room and basked in the breeze that came in from the plains. He looked around at the empty room, glanced at his guitars, then pulled the door shut and went to the motel's lounge.

He found a table near the lobby. The bartender took his time leaving a conversation at the waitress station. Finally, he eyed Doc, dressed in a pair of old cords and needing a shave. He took a breath and came to Doc.

"What can I get you?"

"A shot and a tall, cold beer to keep it company."

The bartender stood there like he hadn't heard Doc.

"My room number is 143." Doc took his room key from his pocket and showed it to the bartender.

The lounge act was a guy in a Navy blue sport coat over a light brown V-neck sweater. A gold medallion hanging from a thick chain nestled among a patch of curly brown chest hair. He sat at an electric piano and talked into a microphone. His voice came from a small amplifier a few feet away. He was reading a dedication of the next tune, which went out to Judy for her 30th birthday.

"Three-oh," the piano man said. "The big one. Or does that come later tonight?"

A trio of women still in their office garb giggled at a table near the small stage.

Doc wondered what Vicki was doing tonight.

The piano man set his computer drummer on a moderate rock tempo, played some introductory chords and sang Billy Joel's "Uptown Girl."

Doc ordered another pair of drinks.

A different man's voice came over the amplifier. It was a familiar voice.

"Ladies and gentlemen, we have a special guest in here tonight. Say hello to Doctor Blues Blevins, sitting down there quietly at the end of the bar."

Doc looked up. The DJ who had introduced him at the concert that night was standing next to the electric piano, microphone in hand. Everybody in the bar looked at Doc.

"Stand up, Doc. Stand up for a minute."

Doc's face was hot. He stood, did a quick scan of the bar, then sat down.

"I guess he's plum tuckered out from his show at The Caravan tonight, folks. I was hoping we could maybe get him up here to sing a song ... Doc?"

Doc grinned and shook his head. He pointed to his throat and mouthed meaningless words that from the other end of the room looked like a good excuse.

"I understand, Doc. Most of these people heard your show tonight. It was a fine one."

The DJ's voice went on and on, just like he was on the radio. Doc stared at his drink. Finally the DJ gave the stage back to the piano man. Doc watched as the DJ went to a table against the far wall.

Sandy was in the chair next to the DJ. He sat down, put his arm around her and gave her a quick kiss on the lips, like he was her husband coming home from a day at the office. A pile of empty glasses glistened in the middle of the table like a fallen chandelier. Sandy lifted her glass and drank whiskey like a kid swigs grape soda.

The bartender brought Doc another whiskey and beer. He gave Doc a big, wide smile. "These are on me, sir. My pleasure."

Doc drank two or three more sets of drinks. People stopped to speak to him as they left the bar. "Liked the show," one man said, his wife clinging to his arm like the floor of the bar was pure ice and she was afraid of falling any minute.

"You kicked ass, brother," said a man in a cowboy hat and blue jeans.

"We bought two of your CDs," said one of the two young women who had sat quietly at a small table in front of the stage, staring at the piano man.

"Thanks." Doc started to tell her it had been a long time between the old records he'd cut on vinyl and the CDs and DVDs today. Started to tell her how the music scene, the club scene, the recording scene, had changed. But he didn't. He smiled and watched the two women walk away.

He'd done some studio work now and then. His name was on a few recordings as a back-up musician. But nothing that anybody would ever find in a record or CD shop in a Denver shopping mall.

Doc held his hand up to the bartender, signaling for another whiskey and beer.

He carried the drinks to his room. He set them on the table next to the bed and hit the television switch but left the volume down. The television's bright light filled the room. A man and a woman sat in the front seat of a car, giving each other serious looks as they exchanged dialogue. He wore a gray fedora and a gray suit. She had on a black dress with a white, lacy collar.

71

It's funny, Doc thought, how the classic black-and-white movie seemed like real history. Even though it was not a true story, there on the television the old film was like an actual scene from the country's past, as though the detective with the shiny black pistol really lived once, really slapped hoods around and sped through the streets in a gleaming black sedan with big whitewall tires and a cigarette hanging out of his mouth. Fiction became truth, almost.

A stray night wind pushed against the window. Doc leaned his head into the pillow. He thought about the first time he knocked on Ike's door. He had the acoustic guitar his father had given him. He leaned his guitar against the wall next to the door on the old wooden front porch and waited for Ike to answer the door.

A white-haired woman opened the door.

"Yes."

"Is Ike here?"

"We're not buying anything."

Ike's voice came from inside. "Who is it?

The woman turned her head and shouted back. "Some kid selling something."

As the television replayed the old black-and-white movie, Doc went over the memory details of that first visit to Ike's. The old woman wore an apron with a bunch of red and green and yellow flowers on a solid blue backdrop. She had white socks rolled down to the ankles. Brown shoes. The smell of chicken broth came out the door. Ike poked his head around the door frame, saw Doc and smiled at him. Half the old man's teeth were black gaps.

"He's not selling anything," Ike said to the woman. He pushed the screen door open. "C'mon in, Doc. Got your guitar? Good. Good."

The room was warm and dark. The woman went down a hallway. Ike motioned for the boy to sit down across from him. The old man sat in the couch and crossed his arms on his belly. He studied the kid.

"You still want to play that thing?"

The boy nodded.

"Look around here. I've been playing music my whole life. Look around this room. This is how I live."

The boy looked at the room. The couch, with worn cushions. Calendar pictures hanging on the wall. A nicked coffee table. A yellow water stain covered most of one wall. In the corner, a small amplifier stood next to an electric guitar.

"This what you want?" The old man said.

What an absurd question, the boy thought. Nobody wants to be poor. Nobody would look at Ike's house and set a lifelong goal to have one just like it.

"Think it over," Ike said.

"I have," the boy said.

"Yeah?" Ike leaned forward.

"I can play this thing," the boy said. "Not as good as you. But someday, better maybe. When I see you at the club, when I hear you play, not much else matters."

"Not even this?" Ike gestured to the room.

"I don't think about this when I play, or when I hear you play."

"What do you think about?"

"About what I'm playin'. That's all."

The old man chuckled. "Me too, Doc. Let me see your guitar."

Ike held the acoustic in his hands, felt the neck, strummed the strings gently. He knocked on the wood. He jerked on the strings and let them go like a rubber band.

"Your father did a good job with this guitar," he said. "My father died when I was five years old. I don't remember much about him." The boy sat opposite Ike and listened.

"Once," Ike said, "when I was a young player and a lot faster on the strings than I am now, I was sitting in with a bunch of guys just in town from the coast. They were playing the Blue Room, a couple blocks away. We went over there after our gig. Man, they could play. But you know what? I stayed with 'em. I started out playing chords behind 'em. Then they gave me a couple leads, and I blew 'em away with my speed. I went up and down the frets. I didn't miss a note.

"Finally, after we'd played for an hour or so, we'd all got lit up with booze, we were jokin' like old hands, this cat says, cool and casual like, he says 'Ike, lemme hear your fifteenth fret D.'

"I said, huh? What D?'

"He said he thought he was out of tune and wanted to check the fifteenth fret D."

Ike rolled his eyes and smiled. "I didn't know what a fifteenth fret D was. I'd played it. But I never knew it. I couldn't read music.

"Man, I was embarrassed. We played a couple more tunes, with me on rhythm, then we left. They were friendly enough, and we played alright together. They invited me back. But I never went back."

Ike stood up. He handed the guitar to Doc.

"Go home and practice this thing just like you've been doin'," he said. "But don't come back here until I can call out every chord on your neck and you can play each one, goin' up the neck and then back down. I want to call out blues scales by letter and have you play them."

Doc heard voices. He sat up in bed. The television screen was still shimmering. He flicked the TV off. Sandy giggled on the other side of the wall. Then there was a man's voice. The wall muffled the words. Sandy laughed again. Something thudded against the wall. Then it was quiet. The soft whisper of a breeze seeping through the door told Doc to sleep.

VI

The diner, a gray cinder brick building about 50 feet off the road, was hooked up to a garage, where a mechanic in striped blue overalls leaned into the guts of a pickup truck. A couple of truckers boomed their horns at each other as they passed on the highway. Across the road, a dirt hill covered with a balding patch of scrub brush and small pines caught the morning sunlight.

"This reminds me of when I was a boy," Doc said between sips of hot coffee.

"How so?" Sandy scanned the pages of a day-old newspaper.

"My father took me fishing. You never realize, when you pass through a place like this here, you're on the road and all you see is plains that reach up to the hills, and then sky beyond that. Up in there are streams and beaver dams and lakes and meadows, places where you can fish for trout and then find a spread of grass to lay down for a nap. My mother used to pack us cheese sandwiches that she'd wrap in waxed paper, along with a couple apples and bananas and some cookies. They were usually crumbled by the time you got around to 'em." Doc chuckled.

Sandy looked up from her newspaper. "You tell a good story, Doc, you know that?"

"It's no story. It's the truth."

"I know. It's just hard for me to imagine you doing country things."

The counter man, his arms marked with the fading ink of blue tattoos, cleared away their plates and poured hot coffee into their mugs.

"You're the Blues Doctor, urban musician, a creature of the streets and the nightclubs," Sandy said. "You're no fisherman."

Doc peered out the window at the hills glowing red with sunshine. "I was once." He grinned. "A fisherboy. Me and my old man."

"Let's hit the road," Sandy grabbed her purse.

Doc held up his hand. "Let me do this one." He took out his wallet and handed the counter man some bills.

"Contract calls for me to get the meals and the drinks on the highway," Sandy said.

They stepped into the morning coolness.

"Fuck the contract," Doc said. "I felt like buying you a coffee. Let's go buy a fishing pole."

Sandy smiled. She wore deep red city lipstick, neatly pressed blue jeans, a white blouse with cowboy-cut pockets over each breast, and powder on her face. Red canals ran through the whites of her eyes.

"Let's get into town and find a bed," she said. "I'm tired of driving. We've got a rare night off tonight, and I want to get there with some time to enjoy it."

She handed her newspaper to Doc and they climbed into the van.

The road was mostly empty, except for an occasional semi, or a rancher in a dented pickup truck. Fresh air streamed through the open windows of the van's cab.

Telephone poles and fence posts clicked regularly along the side of the road like railroad ties with lots of space between them.

"Would you believe it if I told you I'm a country girl?" Sandy said.

Doc looked at her. "There a reason I shouldn't?"

She shrugged. "No. It's just that you don't know much about me, don't ask much about me."

"I was raised to mind my own business." Doc kept his eyes on Sandy. She watched the road.

"I lived outside of a town in Colorado, Longmont. But we weren't hicks. My daddy was a lawyer who liked open spaces. I grew up with a bunch of farm and ranch kids. Man, I headed for the city the day after I graduated from high school."

"You ever miss it?"

She shook her head, then smiled. "Well, okay. Sometimes. Like when I'm stuck in a traffic jam. Or at night when there's a siren going and somebody's screaming and fighting down on the street, I remember how quiet it was out there. You could hear birds singing. But I was on my own. My daddy spent his life in bars, and when he was home my brother came first. He was four

76

years older than me, and I mean he was my daddy's boy. He could do no wrong.

"Bastard." Sandy's fingers tightened around the wheel.

"So that left you and your mother."

Sandy spit laughter. "My mother? You kiddin? Mrs. Committee Woman herself? Man, she split her entire life between the kitchen, where she baked cookies and pies and cakes for the PTA and the Republican Women's Committee and this function and that party, and the rest of the time she was at meetings, writing proposals, planning teas and speeches and soirees.

"The day I hit the city, I never looked back. I don't wanna talk about it."

"How'd you hook up with Dexter?"

Sandy smiled. Her grip on the wheel loosened. "Dexter. I dunno. I guess at a bar. Yeah. Somebody from the office where I worked knew somebody who worked for him. We got introduced at a bar one night. We sat next to each other while some clown at the piano – yeah, that's it, he was in this bar scouting the piano player. Who turned out to be a dud. A big dud. But Dexter sure didn't. I was working for him inside a week, and it's been almost ten years since then."

Doc wanted to ask more. Like what sort of duties her job included besides driving blues musicians from concert to concert around the West. Like how much money she made managing the shows. Like what else did this Dexter fellow do. And was it legit?

"Your life sounds like a blues song," he said.

Sandy chuckled. "That bad?"

"Hey. The blues ain't bad. You gotta have some love and happiness in your life for there to be any blues."

"I guess. Sounds pretty corny though. Like something a country hick might say."

Doc grinned. "Nope. I grew up in the city. Right downtown. After my father ran away, my mother sold our little corner of the suburbs – man, I could've been a little-league kid and a boy scout and the whole bit. We took a walk-up apartment downtown so my mother could be close to work."

"The way you were goin' on back there, I figured you grew up on the banks of a trout stream." Sandy took her eyes off the road and looked at Doc. The sun shone on his gray and blonde whiskers.

"Nope. There's no country in me. My father took me fishin', that's all. I liked going into the hills with him. It was a new place that he showed me, but my home was in the city, just more so after he left. My life really changed then."

As Sandy drove, Doc remembered. The boy returned to Ike's after a week of practice. The old man sat with his electric on his lap, plugged into the small amp a few feet away. He called out chords, and the boy pulled each one out of his guitar with his pick. Up and down the neck of the guitar, he produced D chords, A-flats, F-minors at will. Finally, the old man smiled.

"Good. That's real good. Now play me a twelve-bar blues progression in A."

The boy smiled. This he knew. This was no test. It was a walk. He played a slow-tempo blues.

Ike leaned over his guitar, and with a slow, easy move of his hand made the electric wooden instrument sing a warbly blues line. His fingers hit each note cleanly, bending the strings, coaxing out melodies that came from the amplifier's speaker as clearly as a man's voice enunciating a narrative poem. He rocked back and forth easily, shaking his head as he stretched a note over three or four counts and the music hung in the room like a siren.

Suddenly, Ike picked up the tempo. He played four upbeat measures, then laid the guitar on his lap while his student moved along steadily at the former pace.

"Doc."

The boy stopped in mid-strum.

"Doc. I lost you."

The boy grinned. "I know. I figured you were ad-libbing and we'd come back. I figured the most important thing was to keep the tempo."

"You figured." Ike shook his head. "Well, you figured wrong. Your job is to listen to me and to support me. I'm the lead guitar, you're the rhythm guitar. The drummer keeps the tempo. You understand?"

The boy flexed and shook his left hand. His wrist muscles were sore.

Ike laughed. "Get used to it. This is what we're gonna do for the next month or so."

"Why? What's going on here? You just want me to back you up while you practice? I don't understand."

"Because." Ike's voice was short. He stared into the boy's face as he talked. "Because you can't lead until you know how to follow, that's why."

Ike's eyes narrowed. He gazed silently at the boy as a clock ticked away half a minute on the table next to the couch. Then he smiled.

"You told me you want to be a blues player."

"Yes sir. I do."

"You want my help."

"Yes sir."

"Then listen to me. You play those chords at home, over and over. Play every variation of them you know, in every key. Do that until it's like breathing, until your fingers do it all automatically, without you tellin' 'em to. Do it until you can sit back and listen to the cars go by or a man and a woman fight or while a completely different song plays on the radio and you can listen to it while you keep the blues line going. And there's one more thing I want you to do."

He paused. "Listen."

The room was still. The sound of a spoon tapping against a pot came from the kitchen. A fan whirred somewhere. A breeze pushed through the room and rustled a window curtain.

"Take a half hour each day and just do what we're doing now. Just sit and listen." He grinned and leaned his guitar against the couch. "I mean it. I don't care when you do it, early morning or before bed or lunchtime. But do it.

"I met a man once who was the fastest guitar player I ever saw. He came into a session I was at, and man, his fingers went so fast you could barely see 'em. Blurs of flesh. We had a full house that night, and you should have heard the people clap when he finished his first song. I put my guitar down and clapped too. Then he did it again on the next song. And the next. Just went up and down that guitar like he'd been born with it in his hands. But it all started sounding the same. The man couldn't play slow. He

79

couldn't change the pace. Finally, the session leader decided it was time for the house band to take over. He asked the man to stay up there on the stage and play some rhythm."

Ike leaned forward, like he was whispering a secret.

"Man, I don't like to talk down other players. But this is a fact. The man couldn't play rhythm. He kept throwing solo licks into someone else's lead, tripping up the band, gettin' in the way of everyone else's rhythm. They finally asked him to step down. The man had never learned to listen to other players. He was no musician at all."

Ike's wife came into the living room. She smiled at the boy. "You hungry?"

"What about it? She's been making soup all afternoon. I think she wants someone's opinion of her cookin' besides mine. I like whatever she makes, even when it's not so good." He winked. "Course, she likes whatever I play, too, even when it's not so good."

They went to the kitchen and ate a bowl of vegetable soup with a side plate of saltine crackers.

A semi passed the van, horn blaring, jarring Doc back to the present. Sandy pumped the brakes, then resumed speed.

"Yeah," Doc said as the van skimmed across a plateau and entered a small valley set in dusty, brown hills. The sky was a hazy blue. "I'm a city guy all the way. When I was a kid, I hung out on the street, and I got so I liked the noise and the smell. Cars drivin' by with their radios blaring. You walk into a diner and you can smell the chili and hamburgers. People shout at other people above the traffic."

Sandy nodded. "I guess. That's all a bunch of noise to me. I like the city because there's things to do at night, places to go. Restaurants, any kind of food you want. Night clubs. Any kind of music you want. And I got my work."

"Me too." Doc smiled. "I got my work, except man told me once it ain't work if it's something you like doing. So I guess I haven't worked much in my life."

He leaned his head back and closed his eyes. The next time he opened them, the western sky was a dark pink. The lights of Phoenix were starting to show across the horizon, like a procession of dimly flickering candles. The highway was heavier with traffic. Rock music came from the van's stereo speakers.

"Man," Doc said. "Did I sleep?"

"Yeah." Sandy laughed. "You slept."

He sat up and rubbed his eyes as houses and condos and apartments began to sprout out of the desert. They passed entire communities that were sealed off by white and brown stucco and brick walls. The skyscrapers of downtown fingered into the sky, their windows lit up and twinkling. Sandy drove straight into town and found a parking lot inside one of the high rises.

"A hotel?" Doc said.

"I'm tired of fleabag motels. Our budget's in good shape. Let's live a little."

While Sandy signed them in, Doc found a postcard with cactuses and purple hills and blue skies. He carried his acoustic and electric guitars and left the rest for the bell boy. They left the elevator at the fifteenth floor. A guitar strummed softly from the ceiling speakers in the dark blue, carpeted hallway. Doc stopped outside his door and pushed in the key. He watched Sandy walk away, her blue jeans dusty and tight on her butt.

"Want your back scrubbed?" The loudness of his voice startled him.

She stopped, turned around and looked at him like he was some stranger accosting her on the street.

"It's a joke," he said.

"Oh." She eyed him. "Too bad." She turned away and unlocked her door, then disappeared inside.

It was dim in Doc's room. But it was a nice spread. The dark brown carpet was thick and spongy. He kicked off his shoes and let his feet sink into the pile. A wall cooler whirred. Brown and beige paper with thin designs of flowers and ferns covered the walls. A big mirror behind a brown wooden dresser showed Doc. A small refrigerator was stocked with miniature boozes and mixes and a six-pack of beer.

Doc popped one of the beers open and sat down on the foot of the bed. He drank half of it in a few swallows, toasted his image in the mirror and gulped the rest of it. The beer was cold and strong. He could feel it go down. He sighed and went to the bathroom for a hot shower. He threw his clothes in a pile and turned the water on full. It came out strong and hot and Doc stepped into the tub. The water hit his back like hundreds of warm pin pricks. He stayed in a long time, filling the bathroom with a veil of steam, wrapping himself in the soothing warmth. He came out with a towel wrapped around himself, his skin tinged pink.

Doc went to the window and pulled open the drapes. The lights of the city made a shimmering blanket to the horizon. He pulled an easy chair next to the window, fixed himself a whiskey and water and another beer. He propped his feet on a chair and wrote his postcard.

"Dear Vicki:

"Man, I miss you. I'm in Phoenix. Got the night off. I'm in a hotel room looking at the city lights, thinking about you. Hope you're thinking about me." He signed it Doc.

Then he tore it up and dropped the pieces in the waste basket. He picked up the telephone and dialed Vicki's number.

He wanted to hear her voice. He wanted to tell her what he'd written on the postcard. He wanted to ask about Grady and Maggio's and Vicki's tomatoes and her job and the weather and the other things people who have shared life talk about.

The phone rang eight, nine, ten times. Then a voice: "I'm not in right now. Leave a message."

Doc hung up and looked at the scraps of postcard in the waste basket.

He picked up the phone again and called room service for a hamburger. Then he leaned against the chair, watching the city lights like the window was a big aquarium.

Headlights crawled along the network of streets below. Cars carrying drivers to dinner, to night jobs, to the grocery store, to the bars. Hundreds of strangers passing each other on the streets, paralleling each other on avenues separated by brick and steel and glass. Thousands of people gathered up under the same tower of lights, tied to each other by jobs and families and churches and taverns.

Somehow, it all worked. The cars went their own way, mostly without bothering the other cars. The people went to their offices and homes, to the shopping centers, walking the streets between stops. And they mostly managed to get along. More than a million of them in a few square miles, using the same electricity, sharing the same water, everything connected up by wires and pipes and concrete.

There was a knock at the door, and a man's voice. "Room service."

Doc opened the door, with the towel still wrapped around himself, and he signed the room ticket. He took the hamburger to the table, opened another beer and spread out the sandwich and fries.

He watched the window while he munched on the juicy hamburger. He smiled. There was nothing out there but black sky and lights. The brightness of the city had erased the stars. He washed the bun down with beer.

The booze started to kick in. Doc felt warm contentment. He was on the road. He had a job. He had food. It's funny. Sometimes you drink all night and never feel it, and then you just have a couple some other night and you soar.

He brought the rest of the beer to the table, poured another whiskey and found an electric guitar on the small table radio. He pulled up his seat to the city and watched some more, like someone who sits at a window all alone on a winter afternoon and watches a snowstorm, flake after flake after flake, blow through the air on the other side of the glass.

It's almost like a visual lullaby, the quite parade of traffic moving through a still-life painting of yellow and white light framed by the black edge of a hotel high above it all.

When he was a kid in the city, he used to take his guitar up to the roof of the apartment house. He sat down with a bottle of pop, and he studied the city lights while he worked on his chords under the dim flickering of stars in the sky. Down on the street, voices drifted along the sidewalk, up the walls of the buildings, echoing lightly like noises bouncing through a canyon. Cars trickled by, their engines faint, except for an occasional roar when someone stomped on the gas pedal and screeched away from a stop sign. Up there on the roof, he felt like he was on an island, with an ocean of activity and life around him – radios playing music in half-open windows, men and women sitting next to kitchen windows talking about in-laws and jobs, kids on the street smoking cigarettes and goofing off, people lined up in smoky bars sipping on drinks while voices droned on tinny television sets. Up there, he felt safe and static as everything moved around below him.

That roof, the small apartment he shared with his mother – these were home, until the morning he came in at 5 o'clock smelling of booze and cigarettes after a night of jamming at Jimbo's place. It was a month after his high school graduation. His mother sat at a chair in the kitchen, a magazine open in front of her, and he told her he and a couple of the guys were putting together a band. They'd found a place to rent where they could practice loud without being arrested.

"How will you live? How will you eat? Or is there some millionaire taking care of this for you?"

"A couple of the guys have day jobs. I'm gonna find something part-time. It's a neat place, Mom. You should see it. You will see it. I'll share a room with Ed Blake. He's our drummer. It's got a big living room where we can leave our equipment set up."

She sighed. "You're just a kid."

"I'm 18, Mom."

"Is this really what you want to do with your life? You want to be a musician?"

He nodded. "Yeah. Ike says I can be good."

"Ike Ike Ike. I'm tired of hearing about Ike. Does Ike make a lot of money playing the guitar? Does he have a family?"

"He has a wife. He has a small house. I don't even know if he owns it." The boy took a breath. "Mom. Ike plays the guitar like nobody else."

"And that's what you want to do."

He nodded.

She smiled. At the same time, a tear rolled out of her eye. It was like sunshine on a rainy day.

"At least I'll get some sleep at night," she said. "There's no sense sitting up for you if you're not coming home."

He looked at her, in the chair in her bathrobe, her hair pulled back in a pony tail, her face lightly wrinkled.

84

"You mean you've been up all night?"

"Uh huh."

"Oh, geez. You're right, mom. You need to sleep."

She stayed in the kitchen while he went to his room to pack some clothes. She was still there, in the same chair, with the magazine open to the same page, when he left.

It all seemed so long ago. It had gone by so fast, from then to now, moving from house to apartment house, sometimes living back with his mother in between apartments and jobs, and then in between women. Somewhere in there, it was about ten years ago, his mother died.

He missed her as he sat at the table looking out at the city.

Someone was knocking at the door. Doc took a last look out the window, like something might change if he left, then went to the door and peeked through the peep hole. It was Sandy. He pulled the door open.

Sandy came into the room like a breeze of rose water perfume. She wore crisp, pressed brown corduroys and a red and white patterned shirt that could have been a bandana on a cowboy at the rodeo. She looked at Doc, wrapped in his bath towel, glass of beer in his hand, and she smirked.

"Dressed to go out, I see."

"Just got out of the shower."

She moved past him and sat down on the bed. "I'm going down to the lounge for a drink. You wanna come along?"

Doc glanced at the window.

"You going out later?"

"No," he said. "It just seems like a long time since I've been able to sit and do nothing but think."

"I know. Me too. That's why I thought a drink might be nice."

"Yeah. It might. Give me a minute to find some clothes."

"Okay." She sat on the bed and looked at Doc.

He stood in front of her, thin and small in the big hotel towel.

She stood up. "You mean you want me to leave before you get dressed."

"I didn't say anything. I just thought you might want to."

She glanced down toward his crotch. "I doubt you have anything under there I haven't seen. If you do, maybe I'd like to see it." Her eyes came back up to his face. "Some other time, though. I'll be down in the lounge."

She left. Doc looked at himself in the mirror. His face was red, though he'd been out of the shower at least an hour.

He poked through his bags and found a pair of pants and a shirt. He dressed quickly, then went to the table and gulped the last of his whiskey. He washed it down with lukewarm beer.

He found Sandy at a booth in the back of the lounge. A few men in coats and ties and women in dresses sat scattered at tables in the middle of the room. A couple of lone men were at the bar with drinks in front of them. Hardcore drinkers. Doc knew them from the clubs he had played. They sit at the bar and stare straight ahead, ignoring the music and gab and jukebox and noise all around them, listening to some inner noise or torment or monologue. Doc never could figure out what they were listening to. He'd never been a solitary day-after-day bar drinker. He usually joined customers at their tables, or he drank with other musicians between and after sets, and frequently during.

"You're in a thoughtful mood tonight," Sandy said as Doc sat down.

"Yeah. I am."

The waitress brought him a whiskey and beer.

"That is your drink, isn't it?" Sandy said.

Doc nodded. "Yeah. Both of them."

Sandy picked up a clear glass of pink wine and took a long drink. "What are you thinking about?"

"A little bit of everything," he said. "This all seems to be happening so fast."

"What all?"

"This. I mean, a few months ago, I was in the life I'd been in for a few years. I had my Maggio's job, other money gigs around town. Vicki. I was sort of settled after being unsettled most of my life."

"And now you're unsettled again."

"Yeah."

"And that makes you unhappy."

"No. I'm just not used to it. I was on the road when I was young, and I guess I got most of it out of me then. I'm not used to living in motels, packing and unpacking every day, cheap furniture. All the motel rooms look the same. But ..."

Sandy raised her eyebrows. She motioned to the bar maid for two more.

"But?"

"But isn't this what every musician wants? A concert tour? To be paid to play for people? I like that part of it. I like being up there on the stage and performing for people who have paid to listen to me. I like the applause."

The bar maid unloaded another set of drinks and took away the empties.

"But it isn't like I thought it would be. We're playing small clubs. I don't have any old CDs to sell, just the concert stuff, the studio DVDs Dex and I put together."

"Which are selling like mad." Sandy was already halfway through her new drink. "We took in about five hundred bucks at the Caravan the other night. Part of that's yours, y'know."

"Really?"

She nodded. "I talked to Dexter today. He's barely keeping up with the orders. They're buying them in towns where you've played, and in towns where you're going to play. They've been selling out at some of the club dates."

"That's another thing. I don't even know how long this is going to last. Where I'm supposed to play two weeks from now? How does this work?"

Sandy put her hand on top of Doc's and gently patted his fingers.

"Doc, we're in a different world now. Everybody has a stereo DVD player and big screen flat TVs in their living rooms. They don't buy records anymore. People's tastes change almost overnight. Your music is real popular right now. It might not be next week. Or tomorrow. Who knows?"

"Dexter seems to know."

"He doesn't know. He only knows what's hot today. He has no idea what it'll be tomorrow morning."

"Sure he does. He'll invent it. Isn't that what he's doing with me? Inventing?"

"Sort of." Sandy pulled her hand away and massaged the rim of her glass. "I'd say we're packaging you. Nobody can create a Doc Blevins. But somebody sure as hell can package him and sell him, with the right promotion."

"You mean, like dressing me the way you've dressed me, like making me play certain songs in a certain order, even making me wear this goddam beard."

"Sort of. Yeah. But there's a lot of selling and packaging going on that you never see or feel. Ads. Newspapers. Promotions. Radio play and spots. CDs and DVDs. It all adds up. Believe me, Dexter knows what he's doing."

"I do believe you."

Doc sighed and threw another whiskey down his throat. The room was getting hot. Piano chords hung in the air. The music was everywhere. The bar maid brought one more round.

They sat quietly, working on their drinks. A soft hum of conversation filled the room. The bartender, wearing a red vest over a white shirt and black bow tie, buffed a booze glass on his sleeve and hung it by its stem from a rack above the bar. He took an empty cocktail glass from one of the solitary drinkers, mixed a fresh potion and set it, its ice cubes tinkling, the brown booze wet and glossy, in front of the customer. Like an automatic drinking machine, the man reached out for the glass, lifted it to his mouth, sipped off the top and set the glass back down.

"You're a damn fine guitar player, Doc." Sandy's voice came out of a mist of bar noise.

"Thanks."

"I mean it. That's not groupie talk. You're better than a one-town, smalltime band."

Doc thought about Grady, the house band at the Century Sky Room.

"There are a lot of good musicians out there," he said. "I mean fine musicians. I've played with them. I know."

"I believe you. But you're special, Doc. You got just a little bit more."

"Yeah. Okay. Thanks." He looked at her and forced a smile. His head was going around. It was close in the bar. Makeup covered Sandy's face: red lipstick, a puff of rouge, eyeliner, eye shadow. Her hair glowed with cement or glue or whatever stuff came out of the spray can and made women's hair stand still.

"I'll bet you were one of those guys who wore glasses and stayed inside every day after school, practicing your guitar, while all the other boys were outside playing baseball. I'll bet you could read music by the time you were five years old."

Doc shook his head. "No. I played baseball. I wasn't any good at it. I wasn't any good at any sport. But we used to have some great night football games. We'd go down to the grade school after dark. They had a couple of spotlights shining out on the lawn. We played tackle football, and we played it hard. We ran and laughed and nobody got hurt. You can't get hurt on a field of grass at night."

Doc grinned and shook his head. "It always ended up a big wrestling match. There was this one guy, Barry Hillman. Man, he spent his whole childhood fat. And big. He was always the fullback, and you couldn't bring him down with a solo tackle. We'd pile on him, and he'd start giggling, still plugging forward, pumping his legs, 'til we were just a big pile rolling around on the cool grass. Man, you didn't want the night to end. I'd go home all sweaty and itchy. And I slept all night."

A table on the other side of the bar erupted into laughter. There were more people in the room now. A few empty stools broke up the row of drinkers along the bar like quarter rests in a string of eighth notes.

"Where'd you learn to tell stories?" Sandy reached her hand out and stroked Doc's arm with her finger.

He shrugged. "Ike, I guess."

"Ike?"

"Yeah."

"That the guy who taught you guitar tricks?"

Doc frowned. "There's no such thing as guitar tricks. He taught me shortcuts, like using the bar E-seven if you're already in the fifth fret for an A. But that's small-time stuff."

Sandy's face was a question mark. Like his mother's had been whenever he tried to explain Ike or the guitar.

"Never mind."

"What else did you do when you were a kid?" Sandy was nearly shouting now. A couple of guitarists and a drummer were starting to warm up on a small bandstand in the far corner. Tables of people laughed and shouted jokes and stories.

Doc looked back, searched his childhood for more stories. His mind was an empty computer screen flashing No Find after a word search.

"No more stories," he said. He finished off another beer and set the glass in the middle of the table with a thunk. "And I never wore glasses."

Sandy smiled. "So much for stereotypes."

More drinks appeared on the table. The small combo – a female guitar player with black hair that hung in even strands at ear length; a male bassist with black and gray hair blown back into a curly wave; a kid drummer with pimples and stringy blonde hair that hung in loose bangs on his forehead – opened with a smooth, bossa nova "Girl From Ipanema." The woman sang the lead, landing just on the flat side of each note. The customers drank and talked on.

"Man," Doc said. "This is real depressing."

Sandy nodded. "Maybe more booze would help."

"Uh uh." Doc lifted his glass and chugged the rest of the beer. "An atomic bomb of whiskey wouldn't help this scene." He stood up.

"Where you going?"

Suddenly she was the stern-faced Sandy of back-stage preparations, of long-distance telephone calls with Dexter. Sandy the road boss. "Do I have to tell you?"

She melted back a bit. Her eyes flickered. "No. Of course not. I just wondered."

Doc let out a long breath. "I'm sorry. I guess I really needed a night off. This business of playing the same sets over and over every night, working with a new group of musicians all the time, it's a drag sometimes. I'm going for a walk."

90

Sandy smiled, the warm liquor glow back in her cheeks. "Want company?"

"Thanks. No."

The lobby muted the chatter and music from the bar. A gray-haired woman stood behind the cash register in the hotel's glass-enclosed gift shop. She was surrounded by rows of newspapers and magazines, candy, cards, jewelry and books. She stared out the glass. Her eyes caught Doc's. He nodded to her. She looked away.

Doc went outside and stood on the corner. Cars waited at the light, their sound systems booming electric guitars and pianos, bass drums thump-thumping like an amplified heart beat. The light turned green. Tires squealed and the music faded. Then along came another car, blaring a similar rhythm, stopping at the light. The cruisers came in steady waves, like ocean water pounding on a quiet beach.

City sounds hadn't changed over the years. Doc remembered his roof top when he was a kid, how he could sit up there on any night and listen to the same sounds. Even the sirens lost their urgency and became part of the natural background of the city's soundscape. The city noise was reassuring. Even when you're all alone, there's life out there, people doing things and going places.

Doc walked south. He crossed Van Buren Street, with its endless string of headlights lined up all the way back to the horizon. He turned around and looked at his hotel. Lights piled on top of each other, each of them representing a single unit of life, each of them identical, with its own television, radio, telephone, shower, bed and Gideon's Bible. He tried to figure out which room was his. About halfway up, he saw the black silhouette of a body standing at the window looking out on the city.

Doc wondered if the person was thinking the same kind of thoughts he had been thinking, when he was at a window just like that one earlier, staring at the same city lights.

He walked past office buildings that were sealed up for the night, until he found himself in a residential neighborhood. The houses were small, one-story boxes, with light shining in their windows. Televisions flickered. The sidewalks were still. The only sound was Doc's shoes on the cement.

His mother used to talk to him the way Sandy had. She'd ask him about his day, what he did, why he did it. She used to ask him what he thought about. Questions all the time. It hadn't been like that when his father was there. Then, the three of them talked naturally – or so it seemed, at least, to a little boy. His mother and father kidded around and laughed. Then his father was gone and it was different. She always had to know where he was going, how long he'd be gone, what he was planning for the future.

Finally, he'd leave the house and go for walks. He went to the drugstore and read magazines. He went up on the roof and listened to the city. He went to the parking lot across from The Palmer House and listened to the music and watched the men and women smoking and laughing among the parked cars and painted parking lanes. He went to his room and practiced chords and leads. Or he lay on his bed and listened to the radio, tuning the AM dial until he found a scratchy station from some faraway place like Oklahoma City, where they played different music and talked fast and furious between songs about weather and new music and how the baseball teams did that day.

None of it was really anything worth reporting to his mother. Or to Sandy.

Doc heard organ music. And singing. He stopped. It was a choir. A church choir. The music came from across the street, a cinder brick building painted white. A door was open. Yellow light poured out into a rectangle on the sidewalk. A white streetlight hung in the blackness above the building.

Doc stuck his head in the doorway. At the other end of the green-tiled room, a group of black men and women were lined up in rows, in three tiers. The director, with his back to Doc, talked to them, his voice bouncing through the room.

"Try it again. And basses, remember to listen. Stay with the melody and don't trail. Stay and don't trail. Understand?"

He clapped his hands, counted out four with the tapping of his foot, and the organ player and singers came in together. The organist moved along with choppy chords as the choir sang gospel, the women's voices trembling along the high notes, the men's voices booming below. They all stared at the director, their mouths making big ovals. Doc looked at the organ player, off to

92

the side, the organ perpendicular to the choir and director. He was a kid, maybe 16 or 17, his black hair thick and full. His eyes went from the director's arms to the keyboard.

The director cut off the music. The kid grinned and jumped into a quick honky tonk chicken shack riff. A woman in the front row started clapping her hands to the music.

The director shouted. "Clarence. Clarence. C'mon, now, this isn't rock 'n' roll. Save that stuff for your own band."

The kid pulled his hands back. The music stopped. There was whispering. The director turned around and looked at Doc, who had stepped into the room. He walked quickly toward Doc, his shoes padding across the tile.

"I'm sorry," he said. "This is a closed rehearsal."

"That's cool," Doc said. "I should be apologizing."

The director ushered Doc outside and pushed the door shut.

Doc stood under the streetlight. He could barely hear the organ music through the cinder bricks. In one brief flash, the kid had played a nice piece of blues. Maybe there was hope, Doc thought. Maybe the computer drumming machines and synthesizers wouldn't take over the nightclubs yet.

The night was warm. He walked back toward the hotel. The skyscrapers, though just a few blocks away, seemed distant. They were like a fortress, the way they stood in the air with their lights gobbling up the blackness. A jet winked its red wing lights above the city as it banked toward the airport.

Van Buren was the only street with any life. Hookers and drunks and men with wide, dopey eyes strolled the sidewalk alongside the street. The traffic, stopped at each signal light, was like a river caught in a series of locks, each light taking it to the next level, until it was released into the desert in one direction or to meander into Tempe in the other. A man in a dark gray suit stood on the corner, Bible in hand, and barked a sermon.

"With Jesus as your savior, you need not fear," he said, walking back and forth, eyeing each car. "Take Jesus into your heart. Invite him into your life. And have no fear."

His voice went out into the traffic and mingled with the revving motors and rap and soul, becoming part of the city noise.

93

Doc crossed the street and moved into the shadows of the skyscrapers, walking along the empty sidewalks, leaving the brightness and life of the main drag behind him. At the next corner, a street sweeper sat in the cab of his machine, smoking a cigarette. He and Doc watched each other as Doc moved quietly across the street, to the next block of cement and glass. Finally, he was back at the hotel.

He stood outside the entrance. Couples crossed the street, arm in arm, and went inside the hotel for a late dinner or drink. Others came out and disappeared into the covered parking lot with rows of cars stacked up into the sky.

When Doc was a kid heading for The Palmer House, people walked the streets. There were apartment houses where you could sit on the front steps with a cold drink on a summer night. Passersby stopped to talk about the weather or the ball game or the economic situation. Men gathered in pool rooms. Neighborhood folks, laborers after work, went to taverns where jukeboxes played music and televisions beamed boxing matches or news shows. Drinkers smoked cigarettes. Clinking glasses and laughter rolled out of the doors onto the streets, where kids leaned on cars listening to their radios and smoking cigarettes.

Now, people parked in a guarded cement tower, rode an elevator to a crossing bridge or pedestrian lane, went into a sealed-off nightclub deep in the throat of a building with doormen, sat and had their drinks and conversation, then went back to their cars and drove far away to some green lot on the outskirts of the city, leaving the streets deserted and quiet.

Doc looked into the bar. The booth where he and Sandy had sat had another couple. They sat close, the man in a coat and tie listening to a woman in an evening dress as she talked, her hands waving in the air. The combo, wearing matching white pants and satiny blue shirts with billowy cuffs and wide, open collars, played some song Doc barely recognized from the radio, something he had heard while tuning from one country station to another for Sandy.

He went to the bar and ordered a whiskey and beer. Man. Here he was, with the solitary drinkers. A place he'd always sworn he'd never end up. He glanced at himself in the mirror. He smiled.

94

The man next to him looked up, saw Doc grinning in the mirror, and he dropped his head back to his drink. Doc tossed down the whiskey and cooled his throat with the beer.

He asked the bartender to send a bottle and a six pack up to his room, set a dollar bill on the bar and left.

He grabbed a free newspaper from a rack by the elevators and thumbed through the pages as the elevator shaft sucked him up the spine of the hotel. It was an alternative paper, full of entertainment and restaurant calendars and club news.

In his room, Doc propped his feet on a chair by the window. He sat next to the glow of city lights and read the newspaper. He came to a page with a picture of himself playing the guitar. It was one of the photos Dexter had put together for the press packet.

The headline read: "Blues legend to play Dooley's."

Doc poured a whiskey, folded the newspaper in half and leaned back to read about himself.

One of the best shows going this weekend will be at Dooley's Friday night, when blues veteran Doc Blevins takes the stage.

This club continues to run away with the bookings in this region, staging one class act after another while the establishment spots book gigs that gag and then some more.

Blevins is hot on the trail of a successful video barrage. He's been playing packed houses – in fact, the Dooley's show may be sold out even as you read this.

Blevins cut his teeth on the guitar listening to old blues cats like Muddy Waters and Howlin' Wolf. He's in the same mold as Little Walter, Lowell Fulson, Buddy Guy, Otis Rush, Magic Sam, with a little Pine Top Perkins, Willie Dixon and Blind Lemon Jefferson thrown in.

The real story here is that he was a white blues musician doing his thing in a world that was dominantly dark. It's no big deal today for white and black musicians to share a stage, but it was a more rare kind of act in the day.

Chicago Slim was the primary architect of Blevins' style. 'He used to play clubs where I hung out,' Blevins says. 'I dug him every chance I got. I thought I knew the blues until I heard him

95

and realized I was only a novice. Slim took me under his wing and taught me how to fly.'

Doc skimmed the words. It was like he was reading about somebody else. Words were there he'd never said, interspersed among a few he had during a hazy telephone interview a week ago.

The story continued:

Slim gave Blevins his nickname. One night, the two guitarists were jamming on stage – now there's a session to catch; imagine those two trading guitar licks on the same tune – when a fan passed out right in front of the stage. The way the story goes, Blevins laid his guitar on the stage floor oh so gently. Slim didn't miss a lick, kept the band and the crowd going, while Blevins tended the fallen fan, got him to his feet and escorted him out into the fresh air. Then Blevins went to the bar and got the man a whiskey, took it out to him and brought him around to a full revival.

He made it back to the stage for the end of the song. And when it was over, Slim went to the microphone and told the crowd they'd just been tended by the good Doc Blevins, the doctor of the blues and the audience too.

The name stuck.

Doc's hands shook. The newspaper rattled as he laid it down. He tossed whiskey into his mouth and poured another. He drank it like water.

The door opened and he was in the hallway. The soft music of the ceiling speakers floated in the air around him. Doc padded along the soft carpet in his bare feet. He heard knocking, banging. He looked and saw himself beating his fist on the door to Sandy's room.

Images sped through his mind. Ike taking the boy's fingers and bending them into chord patterns on the frets, the old man's hands gentle and warm, his arms around the boy's shoulders as he strummed, his voice soothing. Ike bringing him up on stage at the Palmer House, standing there next to him while the kid warmed up for his first on-stage gig with the master. Ike introducing him as Doc Blevins.

The door cracked open. Sandy's face peered out at Doc. He continued to ram his fist into the door. She pulled the door fully open, glanced over her shoulder and stepped into the doorway. She wore a white T-shirt and blue panties.

"What the hell you doing?" she whisper-yelled.

Doc held the newspaper article in front of her face. "No. What the hell are you doing?" His voice boomed through the hallway.

She eyed the article. "What's wrong?"

"What's wrong?" Doc raised his voice louder. "What's wrong? I never knew this Chicago Slim fellow. I backed him once when he came through town on a concert and his rhythm player got sick. That's all. I met the man once. What's this taking me under his wing crap?"

"Shh. Shh." Sandy stepped backward, into her room. "Settle down."

Doc stepped forward, refusing to give Sandy an inch of breathing room. "Where's Ike? Huh? Where the hell's Ike in this story?"

"Doc. Settle down. C'mon in, huh?" She looked over her shoulder again. Doc glimpsed a pair of hairy legs on the end of the mattress.

"Wait," Sandy said. "Gimmie five minutes. I'll come to your room."

"I'll give you one minute." Doc held up a finger. "No more. You got one minute to get your story ready or I'm back here and I'll bust this goddam door down, I don't care who you got in there."

"One minute." Sandy gently pushed the door shut. Doc stared at the closed door for a moment. Up the hall, a door opened and a man's head poked out. His eyes glared at Doc.

Doc went back to his room.

Sandy knocked a minute later.

"It's open."

97

He didn't turn around. He stared out the window and listened to her feet swish across the carpet. She sat down at the table next to him. They both watched the city for a minute.

"Now." Sandy's voice reminded Doc of a receptionist in a dentist's office. All business. "What's the problem?"

He turned and studied her face. Clean of makeup, her hair brushed back, she was like somebody new. Her eyes were wide, alert, and blue.

"You still don't know?"

"I know you're upset about some damn fine publicity work. Why?"

He spread the newspaper on the table. "Most of this is lies. I never knew Chicago Slim. Ike was my teacher, my main man. I told you about Ike."

"You told me you used to listen to Chicago Slim."

"I did. I did." Doc sighed. Maybe she really didn't understand. "What's this shit about how I got my nickname? That story's a total fabrication."

Sandy smiled. "But it's a good story. C'mon, Doc. Look at most blues musicians' nicknames. Do you really know how that Howlin' Wolf guy got that nickname? And what about Muddy? Where'd that come from?"

"I don't care where their names came from," Doc said. "I just care about me and my name. And I told you where my name came from."

"Yeah. Put that story in the newspaper trying to sell tickets. Some old guitar player called you Doc for no reason whatsoever, he just thought it was cute. You'll put the readers to sleep. I'm sorry, but nobody even knows who Ike is."

"My music sells tickets."

Sandy grabbed Doc's whiskey bottle. "You mind?"

She poured whiskey into a clear plastic cup and took a couple of gulps.

"Doc. I know you're a good guitar player. But like you've told me a few times now, the world's full of good guitar players. I've learned from Dexter. The trick is to sell your good guitar player. That's what Dex and I are doing. We're selling our guitar player. And we're doing a damn good job of it. In the big picture,

Doc, how you got your nickname is just part of the folklore of the blues, like Robert Johnson making a pact with the devil if he could be a good guitar player. Do you believe that story? No. It's just a story. We've given you a bigger, better image than you had before. I know Ike's important to you. A year from now nobody's going to remember the story about where your name came from. You can tell your own story. Don't you understand what's going on here?"

"I understand that somebody, you or Dexter, is putting lies in the newspaper about who I am and what I am."

Sandy sighed. Already her cup was empty. She poured another.

"Doc, it ain't like it was a few years ago. Everything's faster now. Less personal. You don't have years to build up a following and establish yourself. You've got months at the most maybe, weeks, before the public becomes interested in something else and moves on. Right now, we've got an audience interested in Doc Blevins. You. Now. We've got to cash in, you've got to do it now, while you're hot."

She touched Doc's arm. "Look. I know where you're from. Your friends know it. The people around you know who you are and what you are."

"Yeah. They're readin' trash like this, they're lookin' at the DVD, and they're sayin' look at Doc. The asshole sold out." He looked at Sandy. "And I didn't sell out, man. I didn't."

"Doc. This is going to be over before you know it. You'll go back to your routine, except with some money put away. And more famous. That's going to help you. The main thing now is you get up on that stage every night, you play your own music. You're still doing that. All the publicity can't change how or what you play. And you're making them happy. Why don't you just let us sell you and you do your thing. Okay?"

The city lights were starting to blur. Sandy's voice was soft and soothing. Doc leaned his head back. She emptied her cup and set it on the table.

Doc barely heard her move away. The door clicked shut. He stood up, turned off the light switch and lay down on top of the bed blankets.

He thought about the pair of legs he'd seen in Sandy's room, the swish of her breasts behind the T-shirt she wore at the door. He remembered sitting on the roof of his apartment building as a kid. It was nearly midnight. His mother had gone out. He couldn't sleep. It was a breezeless Saturday night, with radio music blowing through the air, car doors slamming shut, engines revving, televisions blaring. The air hung in the street like a wet sheet. Headlights came from around the corner. The car stopped in front of his building. The lights blinked off. He peered over the edge, down onto the street. The car, a long, white sedan, sat a few feet behind the stoop. He heard the giggle of a woman. Behind the windshield, arms entangled, a hand went to a breast. He saw his mother's nipple, saw her arm go around the man's neck, listened to the car engine idling while the man and woman embraced.

Doc pulled a pillow out from underneath the bedspread, turned on his back and stared at the soft white reflection of light on the ceiling. Far away, a car horn honked. Then the room was quiet.

VII

A Doc Blevins guitar riff blew out of the speakers that hung in adjacent corners in the small studio. It was like sitting inside a set of stereo headphones. The high hat clomped every second and fourth beat. Doc's guitar bleated along the top of a searing bass and rhythm line.

The disc jockey, in a white, wide-collar shirt, slumped in his chair, which was in the middle of the speakers precisely at the point were left meets right. He was clean shaven, with black hair that curled tightly over thick horn-rim glasses.

The disc jockey turned a knob. Doc's guitar faded away. He pulled the boom microphone into his face.

"Okay. That was some more Doc Blevins for ya, a cut from his concert tour. We got Doc live in the studio. He's in town for two shows at the El Rey Theater tomorrow."

The disc jockey's voice was deep, but soft. Sort of like those voices on the classical music stations, people who sound like they should be from England, except they don't have the accent. This guy was smooth and hip.

Doing the show was Sandy's idea. She said ticket sales were down.

"That's the advantage of bringing the local radio stations into the concert, that's why I'm here on the road with you lover man," she said. "You got built-in advertising. You buy an ad, they play it when they want, in the middle of the night or whenever. But you make them part of the action, they'll promo the hell out of the show, even during drive time. It's worth the cut, believe me. And they get a chance to sell themselves and put their disc jockeys up on stage. Just like using the local musicians for backup brings in their fans. You start with an audience base already in place, and it works for everybody."

Doc nodded. Sandy and Dexter had it all figured. They were like butchers who knew exactly where to trim the fat, leaving just enough to juice the steak and no more.

"His first gig'll be at 8," the disc jockey said. "For you night owls, he'll be back at 10. The doctor is sitting with me now. Got a

101

question about the blues, call it in. You're at 89.9 on the FM side of the tuner. You've joined the Blues Brigade. And I'm Clifford." Clifford stared into the control board as he talked.

"Doc, you've been in the business, what, four decades now?"

Doc chuckled, looked up at the ceiling and counted fingers. "I lost track of the years somewhere along the way, Cliff."

"Yeah." Cliff gurgled a soft laugh and smiled into the mike. "A lot of us did. But since you bring up the years, Doc, that's sort of the point of my question. How has the music scene changed over the past few decades?"

"Geez." Doc leaned back in the swivel chair. "That's like asking me to summarize the weather patterns of North America during the last half century. I guess the biggest change is electronics. The things we can do with electronics and machines. You can get some amazing sounds out of an electric guitar. They got electric drums now. Electric pianos and synthesizers, all thanks to the rockers y'know."

"What about you? How has it changed for you?"

Doc scratched his head. "I don't know. It's been a long time since I've been on the road. I can tell you one thing. Musicians are a lot more sophisticated now. A lot more knowledgeable in different kinds of music. I've played with country boys on this tour who could play jazz and calypso if you asked 'em. A lot of 'em are college educated. They went to school to learn how to improvise."

Doc laughed. "Do you dig that? Figure it out. How do you teach someone to improvise? I don't know. And they teach 'em theory now. I don't know what that means. Theory."

He smiled at the disc jockey.

"When I was learning, we didn't talk theory or improvisation. You maybe heard the word technique if there was enough booze around. I learned my scales, I learned my fills and I learned my color chords and leads. Most important, I learned how to follow other musicians and how to play what's in here."

Doc touched his breast.

"So you read music, Doc?"

"No. If I got one word of advice to people who want to play music, it's learn to read. Man, it's nice to put a chart in front of somebody and they can take it from there."

"We're talking to Doc Blevins, blues doctor virtuoso, and you've got the Blues Brigade." Cliff punched a button. Doc's guitar came out of the speakers. "Here's a piece Doc's performing on his current tour. Got the blues? Got a question for Doc? Call us up."

Cliff hit the volume dial and filled the small studio with Doc. He unscrewed the lid from a square bottle of whiskey and topped off Doc's Styrofoam cup. He poured himself a drink and stuck the bottle at the end of the control board, out of sight. From the hallway window they looked like two men sipping coffee.

A red light on the telephone blinked. Cliff picked up the telephone receiver.

"Hey. What's up?"

He turned his back to Doc and spoke softly into the telephone. A few words came Doc's way between his own guitar riffs. "Another hour or so. Yeah, me too. Not tonight. No bread." A chuckle. "For sure." Clifford hung up the phone and spun around to face Doc.

"Excuse me."

"She's more important." Doc grinned.

"Yeah, well. It's a long story. I wanna see her and I don't. You understand? She's a phone groupie. We went out last weekend. Now she wants to do it again. I'm not so sure."

Doc nodded. "I know."

"Yeah. Of course. You get a lot of groupies?"

"Not on this tour. Man, this is the strangest gig. We go from motel to motel, stay one, maybe two days. When I was on the road before, we stayed in a town until we played it out, then we moved on to the next one. The women hung out in the clubs and sort of attached themselves to each musician, you know, like they'd stake their claim our first night in town and they stuck until we left. This time around it's a lot different."

"Welcome to the big time."

Doc swished whiskey in his mouth and handed the cup to Clifford for a refill.

"You got a nice gig here, looks like."

Clifford shrugged his shoulders. "It's okay. It's a job."

"You got your own show. Your own listeners. You get paid. I don't see you wearing a necktie. I don't see a playlist in front of you."

"Oh, yeah, as far as it goes I've got a damn fine job. I don't get the big bucks the top-40 clowns get, I like the hours. Yeah, I wear my jeans. I don't have to blow dry my hair, I don't have to go to the malls and put up with a bunch of screaming pre-teens. Yeah. I guess I've staked out a nice little niche for myself. I pay the rent, and I play what I want to play. I guess I decided some time ago that was more important to me. For now, anyway.

"Course, I don't know what I'm gonna do when retirement time rolls around." Clifford grinned. "That's something I've started thinking about lately."

"I dig." Doc nodded. "I had a pretty good situation myself, before I went out on tour. I had my own stage and my own regular audience, sort of like you."

Doc looked at the memory, at the row of men and women huddled over their drinks in the small restaurant lounge, at the packed house in the Century Sky Room. He remembered going home to Vicki in the still of the morning. The only sound in the apartment was sleep. Sometimes he'd sit on the couch and have a last drink. Or he'd curl into Vicki and wake up after her the next morning, with the apartment to himself, and she'd left the coffee maker on and he could smell the fresh coffee.

"You get in habits," Doc said.

Cliff brought the volume of the speakers back down. "Okay. We're back with Doc Blevins, who's talking the blues and answering your questions tonight. Doc, I've been reading your bio. You've played with a lot of the blues legends. Who had the biggest influence on your style?"

A picture of Ike flashed in Doc's mind. The old guitarist sat in his living room. He chuckled at a lead Doc had blown and shook his head. He coaxed the boy on, urged him to try again. "Let your fingers feel what's inside of you; let 'em find their way. You know the notes, you know your way around the strings. Just let it come."

104

Doc leaned toward the microphone. Cliff motioned for him to lean back and talk naturally.

"There's a whole bunch of influences," Doc said. "Muddy, of course. Sunnyland Slim. The Howlin' man. Sure, there's pianists in there too. Horn men. They're all in the mix, they're all people I listened to when I was young. Django. Ike Mann."

There. Doc grinned. He got Ike in there. Ike was on the airwaves. He was part of the blues legend now. His name was tossed into the pot with the others. Let the music historians track him down, those people who spend their lives writing journal theses on long-lost political causes and painting styles and musical influences.

The telephone light went on. Clifford picked up the receiver. His left hand was on the kill switch. He had three seconds between the utterance of an obscenity and the time it came on the air to slice the voice off with an electronic knife.

"I have a question for your guest." The voice was soft, a voice that wore glasses and slacks and spent long afternoons studying in libraries.

"Shoot," Clifford said.

The voice came out of the speakers all around Doc.

"Mr. Blevins. I'm enjoying immensely the music I'm hearing on the radio tonight. But I can't find a discography on you. I'd like very much to study your list. I'm a fan of the blues and I've collected the works of a number of players. But I'm afraid I can't find yours."

Four seconds of empty air space filled the studio. Finally, Doc took in a breath and spoke. "I haven't recorded very much," he said. "Mostly on smaller, local labels."

"I see. Could you name one or two for me?"

"Not off hand, I can't. Most of them are out of business now anyway."

"Pity," the voice said. "I really do like what I'm hearing tonight. I'm fascinated by your style, by your command of slide and chording technique."

Clifford rode in like the cavalry. "Sorry, but we've got to move on," he said. "Thanks for your call."

105

"Wait," the voice said. "Who was the bluesman your guest mentioned?"

Clifford looked at Doc, a question mark on his face.

"The last one," the voice said. "You were listing some of your influences."

"Ike Mann?"

"Yes. That's it."

"Obscure," Doc said. "Needs research."

"I'll say," the voice said. "Thanks."

The dial tone buzzed in the studio. Doc sighed. Drops of sweat beaded on his forehead, despite the cool breeze of the air conditioning.

Clifford punched up another song on the CD, filling the room with Doc's blues.

"Sorry about that one," he said to Doc.

"It was a fair question."

"That guy's a real asshole. I recognized his voice the minute I heard it. He's a self-appointed music professor. He does that anytime I've got someone in here, he calls in and starts asking them off-the-wall questions, discussing music theory with 'em. I finally just have to interrupt him and tell him to get off the phone."

Clifford laughed. "Once, right on the air, I told him to get a life, man. Oh, man, I got in trouble, had to do an on-air apology. But it was worth it. He's a real drag."

Doc nodded, took a fresh cup of whiskey and swallowed a big gulp.

Sandy was waiting in the van when Doc came out. The engine was running. Eric Clapton's guitar poured out of the open window, spilling onto the parking lot.

"You ready to boogie?" Her eyes were lit up like neon.

Doc climbed in. He turned down the radio and leaned back against the seat.

"I'm getting old," he said. "I'm beat. I feel like I should go home, put my feet up, have a stiff drink and watch television."

Sandy drank from the whiskey bottle and handed it to Doc.

"That'll perk you up." She giggled. "Better take a drink. We got a jam session to go to."

Doc nodded. He drank the whiskey like it was medicine. The elixir of life was what it was called in a song. Sandy had told him about the jam session earlier, an effort to sell a few more tickets for tomorrow's show. Clifford had mentioned it a couple of times on the radio.

"You sounded great," Sandy said.

The night air blew through the front seat, brushing against Doc's face. He sat up and took another shot of booze.

"Who was that jerk at the last?"

"I don't know. The disc jockey said he was some asshole who always calls up and hassles his guests."

"You did fine." Sandy reached across the seat and touched Doc's knee.

"You been out on the parking lot all that time?"

"Yep." She nodded. "Me and this." She patted the bottle. Sandy drove into the throat of the city, lined with rows and stacks of neon and office lights. They passed through downtown, a sanctuary of cement and glass that seemed almost like a photograph it was so still, and they came out on the other side.

Sandy pulled into a parking lot. A square building, painted in flowing arcs of yellow and blue and purple and red and green, like a 1960s psychedelic bus, sat at the back of the lot. Black asphalt filled with gleaming chrome and black wheels surrounded it. They found a parking spot and Doc grabbed his guitar case from the back of the van.

People gathered around the open front door like foam sudsing up from the spout of a fresh bottle of beer. A bass guitar pulsed through the walls, surrounded by a chorus of electric guitars and pianos, the steady zing of a cymbal. The words painted above the front door said the name of the place was Warsaw Wally's. Home of the Blues.

Sandy and Doc stepped through the crowd. A row of jeans-clad butts hung over a line of bar stools. To the left, men and women in T-shirts played pool and pinball in the game room. They displayed the works of tattoo artists on their arms and shoulders. A woman leaned over a side-pocket 9 ball shot, her breasts hanging inside her v-neck shirt like a cow's udder. A red rose was etched about two inches above her nipple. She looked up, saw Doc watching her, grinned and stroked the cue ball into the 9. It fell into the pocket with a thud.

To the right, a six-man blues band filled a long, narrow stage in front of a wall done in cheap, eighth-inch wooden paneling held up by haphazard rows of big-headed gray nails. Doc pushed through the crowd and found a small table in a corner of the room. He leaned his guitar against the wall. Sandy appeared next to him. A line of men trailed her like dogs picking up the scent of a bitch in heat.

"This seat taken, sailor?" She grinned at Doc. Her teeth were white and straight. Her complexion underneath the makeup was clean. She could have made somebody a fine secretary, in a knit Navy blue suit and white blouse, with tiers of accountants and lawyers and office managers telephoning her for lunch and after-work drinks. Maybe she did that once, until she figured out that jeans and booze felt better than nylons and coffee.

Doc grinned and picked up Sandy's game. "What's a girl like you doing in a place like this?"

Sandy gave him a look of mock shock. "What, you think the place is too nice?"

She laughed. "I got some drinks on the way."

Doc nodded. Sandy's hand landed on his thigh. A woman in black slacks, her hips and upper legs straining at the seams, her hair a pile of blonde curls on top of cheeks and lips painted red, brought a tray of drinks. She set a tumbler of whiskey and a couple of long-necks in front of Doc and gave Sandy two white wines.

Sandy lay a twenty into the serving tray.

Doc leaned back and watched the band. It was fronted by a tall, thin harp player with stringy blonde hair that hung like mop strands over his wire-rim glasses as he bent and swayed to the music, chirping on his harmonica behind the lead guitar's licks, then sucking and blowing deep-throated blues when the solo came his way. Behind him, a bass player in a blue work shirt and a scraggly black beard that made him look like a Franciscan monk plucked his way up and down the electric frets. A sax player stood off to the side, bending over his golden horn that curved into his body like a woman backing into her man in bed. On the opposite side of the stage, the lead guitarist stood next to the electric keyboards. The guitarist in this band clearly was secondary to the harpist and sax man, who tossed the leads back and forth like a game of musical tennis. Behind a bank of toms and cymbals, the drummer, wearing his hair in a thick black pompadour, strode a brisk 4/4 swing with his brushes, his bass drum throbbing at the bottom of the song.

"What ya think?" Sandy squeezed Doc's thigh.

"Your average roadhouse blues band. But the harmonica player's kinda good."

"Yeah. That's what the jockey down at the station told me when I asked a good place for you to play around."

"What is it with you and disc jockeys?" Doc took his gaze away from the musicians and looked at Sandy.

"What do you mean?"

"Nothing. Never mind."

Dancers filled the floor, moving in a general up and down motion in time to the music. Slacks and sport coats and pant suits mixed with jeans and cowboy boots.

"I guess I'm wondering why you're traveling the country with a seedy old blues player, hangin' out in places like this, instead of working in some secure office waiting to meet a good man." Doc finished his whiskey and motioned to the barmaid for more drinks.

"There are good men everywhere," Sandy said. "Except the offices. Those guys are boring. Don't you agree? I mean, look at you."

Sandy lifted her second glass of wine to Doc. "You're not in an office. You're a good man, aren't you? Why aren't you stacked up in a skyscraper downtown bringing home a steady paycheck?"

Doc nodded.

"I grew up bored," she said. "My daddy was always away on business. And when he was home, he was doing something with my brother – scouts baseball, basketball – or he was curled up with a bottle. My old lady did nothing but her committee work and watch TV. My town's idea of a hot Saturday night was going bowling after the little league baseball game. We had one nightclub, if you wanna call it that. A pizza joint that served beer and had a jukebox. The idea of a career in that town was to open your own insurance office. Man, the day I got out of high school I put that town in the rear view mirror of the car my daddy bought me, and I never looked back."

"You didn't want to go to college? Get a career?"

She shrugged her shoulders, poured wine into her mouth and smiled. "I got a career. Dex pays me pretty good money, and I don't have to set my alarm for 6 o'clock in the morning."

Doc decided Sandy sounded like a verse to one of the country western songs she always listened to.

The music stopped and a voice boomed through the room. Doc looked toward the stage. The harmonica player stood at the microphone.

"We got a special cat in the audience tonight. You may've heard of him. He's on a concert tour right now and will be at the El Rey tomorrow night. I'll bet if we all put our hands together we might get 'im up on the stage for a tune. Doc? Doc Blevins, you out there?"

People's heads turned.

Doc snorted. "Bunch o' drunks," he said to Sandy.

"Go," Sandy said. "We can probably sell out the concert tonight."

Doc reached for his guitar and headed for the stage. An aisle formed through the middle of the dance floor. He stepped into the rolling smoke that gathered in the spotlight in front of the drummer. The waitress followed in Doc's wake, and she set a tall glass of straight whiskey on top of an amplifier.

Doc grinned at the band members. The harmonica player crossed the stage and shook his hand.

"I'm Bullet Bob," he said.

"Hi." Doc held his guitar in his left hand and took the harp player's hand with his right.

"We'll start with a 12-bar in E. Just pick it up when you're ready," Bob said.

Doc nodded. He turned toward the band's lead man, plucked the E string and tuned his guitar.

He looked out over the dance floor at the full bar, the rows of drinks glistening like a line of jewels along the long counter. He picked up the glass tumbler and filled his mouth with whiskey, swishing it around his cheeks and swallowing.

Doc blinked his eyes. In front of him was the shimmering dance floor of The Palmer House. Tables covered with white table cloths surrounded the wooden floor.

Cigarette tips glowed like radio tower lights. Ike sat in a folding wooden chair a few feet away, the black chord of his electric guitar wriggling toward the small amplifier.

Ike bent over his guitar, strummed his fingers across the strings, and an E chord filled the room.

The kid pulled an A out of the upper E string and bopped in and around the dominant melody notes for 12 bars. Then he stepped back, picked up the rhythm and listened to Ike take the lead.

It was just like they'd practiced. Except more. This was no living room in the broad sunlight of afternoon with a lazy dog barking at flies in the front yard. This was the dance room of The Palmer House, full of blues fans accustomed to Ike's band, and he was the new kid, and a white one at that, taking his first musical steps at a renowned blues house.

Ike accompanied himself as he sang. Doc went along with a soft background rhythm.

"Oh, mercy, mercy, mercy." Ike hung on each note like it was a guitar string he was stretching out across a couple of bars. He turned his head and grinned at Doc. His guitar followed along a third of the way up the scale. The kid laid down a flawless chord pattern.

Doc closed his eyes and remembered what Ike had taught him. He played the guitar like a blind man because Ike had insisted that he learn the entire neck by feel. And after that he had to play it even one step beyond memory; he had to play the guitar like he breathed. That way, Ike said, he could concentrate on singing. And listening. And, one day, leading.

He landed on a blues note that's not even a flat or a sharp, but just beyond, the string bent into a musical realm that you feel instead of hear.

"Oh yeah," came from the audience. A lone voice of approval from a cat who knows and feels the blues, a cat who

111

works from 7 in the morning until 4 in the afternoon and then sits on a wooden front porch with a cold can of beer that he sips and that helps him get by the next hour of his life and he doesn't really worry about the days and weeks and years beyond that because he's got more beer in the fridge and he's got his porch swing and his cool blades of grass bending in the evening breeze right now.

"Have mercy, mercy, mercy, baby."

Doc answered the words with his guitar, echoing them, sliding and bending the notes until his fingers were nearly fluid, pliable, part of the strings.

"Oh, mercy, mercy, mercy, me."

Ike's voice became Doc's. As the musicians brought the tune to its leaving off place, Ike peered across the still, hot dark air of the room at the kid. The old bluesman winked and did a fadeaway.

Doc blinked again, grinned, stepped back from the edge of the stage and studied the place. The bright room, the spots, the cigarettes, the glowing pinball machines, the white neon tubes dangling above the shining green felt of the pool tables, it all blared at him as the audience broke into applause. Bullet Bob came across the stage and put his arm around Doc.

"Man, you got it, you still got it," Bullet Bob said. Doc answered quietly. "I hope to hell I still got it, kid. I never didn't have it."

He went back to the table and sat down with Sandy's empty glass. He propped his guitar against the corner and stretched back to enjoy the free whiskey and beer headed his way. A line formed at the end of the bar to buy tickets to the El Rey theater for Doc's show the next night.

On the stage, Bullet Bob puffed on his harmonica, his cheeks bulging like a bullfrog's throat as he moved the silver horn up and down his lips. Doc propped his feet on Sandy's empty chair and closed his eyes.

The harp player was good. He breathed blues music into the harmonica and then sucked it back into his lungs. Doc was considering asking Bullet Bob to sit in at the El Rey the next night when a voice poked at him from above.

"Where's the lady who was sittin' here?"

Doc opened his eyes. A man in a jean jacket and blue jeans, his ragged beard hooked to a shiny bald head, stared down at Doc.

"You seen the woman who was sittin' here?"

Doc shook his head. "But if you see her, send her my way, will you?"

The man glared at him and then was gone. Moments later, Sandy came to the table.

"Some bald-headed guy's looking for you," Doc said.

"I know. I've been trying to avoid the son of a bitch." Her eyes flashed. "He's high on something strange."

The bald man came up behind her. He whispered into her ear. Sandy laughed and let the man pull her away, off to a forlorn dance somewhere.

Men and women embraced on the dance floor, shuffling their feet in time to a slow, wandering song that Bullet Bob led with a banshee moan. People sat at tables, pulling on cigarettes, buzzing along on booze and whatever else they'd stuck in their heads and bodies to help them through another night. Pool balls clicked and pinball machines bleeped.

It was like the small ash from a cigarette tossed into a patch of dry prairie grass when the fight started. A flash Doc caught in the corner of his eye. He knew right away and started for his feet. The thing spread quickly through the club. He saw Sandy pounding at the chest of the bald-headed man; a spot of blood stained the top of his head like a splotch of ketchup dropped in the middle of a hamburger bun.

Then that picture spun away and the next one dropped into focus, a woman swinging a beer pitcher into the face of another woman, spraying the place with blood. Bodies tumbled on the floor. Men shouted. Women screamed. Somebody yelled into a microphone for the police, for security, for you people to stop this thing, stop it now. The general tide of the thing pushed Doc toward an emergency exit by the stage. He burst through the door like water pushing through a dam's flood gate.

The parking lot was suddenly cool. Doc watched the boiling madness in the bright light of the club. People wandered out of it, escapees from a blaze, shaking themselves, carrying drinks, leaning back against the dumpster to watch the fight inside as it

113

wore down and more stragglers wandered outside, refugees from a blues bar brouhaha. The police cars came in a whirl of flashing lights and blaring sirens. The men in brown uniforms and shining belt buckles and flat trooper hats extinguished the thing.

Doc heard the voice of a woman, a neighbor to the club. It came from the other side of a cinder brick wall, from the backyard of the house next door. He saw the woman's gray head, and above all the tumult he heard her say that she had enough of this. "I'm calling my councilman tomorrow. I want this goddam rat trap closed permanently."

Sandy stood next to Doc. He looked down at his left hand, flexed his fingers. His hand felt empty.

"Oh my God." Doc went back toward the smoldering scene. He pushed through the crowd. A uniform stood in front of him.

"My guitar," Doc said.

The uniform stepped aside.

Doc found his guitar in the corner where he'd left it. The neck was broken off, dangling, held to the body of the guitar only by the strings. He picked the thing up and carried it back to the parking lot. He took it around to the front of the building, where Sandy was waiting in the van. He laid the guitar in the back, climbed into the van, and Sandy drove them away.

"We'll get you a brand new one first thing in the morning," she said. She took a silver pocket flask from the glove compartment. "Here, take a drink."

Doc shook his head. Headlights came at him in a blur.

"Goddam jerk," Sandy said. "He kept coming at me, coming at me." She unscrewed the flask, tipped her head back and poured booze down her throat. "I guess I shoved him a bit too hard, the crazy son of a bitch. Pushed him right up against some other dude, who pushed him back toward me." She laughed. "Shit. He was like a pinball, going one way and then the other, 'til he finally swung out and hit the first thing going by."

Doc stared straight ahead through the windshield as the van pushed against the night.

Sandy cackled and took another drink. "We'll get you a better guitar," she said. "A brand new one."

They pulled into the parking lot of the motel. Sandy turned the ignition off. The engine sputtered, hacked and died. The whole world was quiet.

Sandy reached her hand across the gearshift knob and lay it on Doc's knee.

"How much those things cost?"

"That one was free," Doc said.

"Free?"

"A gift."

"Shit. I'm sorry."

Her hand went lightly up and down Doc's leg.

"You know why I pushed that guy away tonight, don't you?"

Doc shook his head. He gazed into the dashboard.

"I had plans for tonight. Involving you."

Doc looked up. He watched as Sandy took a swig of booze. He could hear the sound of her throat swallowing. She looked at him.

"I'm sorry about your guitar," she said.

Doc shrugged his shoulders. "It was an old thing."

"C'mon in." Her fingers squeezed the soft spot above Doc's knee. "We'll forget about guitars and bars and concerts for one night."

She leaned across the seat, put her fingers under Doc's chin, turned him toward her and kissed him. Her lips tasted like liquor. She smelled like perfume and cigarettes. She pulled away, trailing the scent of sour alcohol.

"C'mon."

"No."

"Huh?"

"I'm tired," Doc said.

"So. We'll sleep."

"No." He sighed, turned his head and peered out the window. "I'm not interested Sandy. Not like that. Not now at least."

Sandy pulled her hand away.

"Get out." Her voice trembled.

Doc opened his door. The dome light filled the van with a soft, white haze. Sandy's eyelids were heavy with eye shadow. Clumps of mascara clung to her eyelashes. Rouge blushed her cheeks. Her lips were set together in a frown.

"Maybe I'm just tired, Sandy. Maybe I'm missing Vicki."

"Drop it Doc." Her voice rose as she glared at him through the open window. "I don't wanna hear any of your shit. You blew it, big time."

"I'm going to bed Sandy." Doc slid the back door open and grabbed the broken guitar. He carried it across the parking lot, toward the motel. He went around the corner of the building, underneath a metal stairway.

"Don't say no to me, Doc." Sandy screamed. Her voice was at least an octave higher. "I turned someone down for you. You son of a bitch. There won't be a lot more nights. This tour is almost over for you Doc! Get back here!"

Doc slipped the key into the door and stepped into his room. He pushed the door shut with his foot and stood in the darkness for a moment. He held the broken guitar close. Outside, a car door slammed. Footsteps crossed the parking lot. They clomped up the stairway and down the cement walkway above him. A door creaked open and slammed shut.

Doc opened the door and looked up and down the sidewalk, then went into the parking lot. The moon shone on the pavement, which sparkled like a field of black snow.

He carried the guitar to the dumpster and carefully dropped it on top of a pile of newspapers and paper bags. He stood back from the dumpster.

"I'm sorry, Ike. I should have taken better care of it. I should have done more with it. It was a fine guitar."

Back in the motel room, Doc sat at the small round table next to the window. The lights were off. Moonlight glowed on the drapes. He listened to the quiet. He remembered when Ike died. The old man had come down with a cold. Then it was the flu. It lingered.

The boy stopped by for a visit one afternoon. The old man was in bed, propped up by pillows. White spikes of whiskers

116

covered his face around his beard like needles marching across the smooth, green stern of a desert cactus. His face was thin.

"How's your practice, Doc?" That was always Ike's first question.

"Fine."

Ike grinned. "Good. Good."

They sat in the sick room. Afternoon sounds drifted in through the half-open window. A truck wheezing through its gears a few blocks away. Voices of children playing in the dirt in a dusty back yard. A table radio somewhere played organ music. Ike's wife knocked silverware against a pot in the kitchen, followed by the sound of stirring. You could smell the chicken soup in the house, and the mentholatum, and the sickness.

Ike breathed through his mouth, a steady, long passage of air in and out.

"They can't figure out what this is," Ike said. He looked at the ceiling as he talked. "All I know is, it won't go away. One minute I am hot and sweaty, the next minute I'm shivering and hollering at the old woman for a blanket."

He stopped and took a couple of breaths. "I tried to get up the other day. Went out to the couch. I held my guitar, but I couldn't play it. Couldn't even bend the strings."

He shook his head. "I don't think I'll be playing it any more."

"Ike. I …" The boy didn't know what to say. He knew Ike was dying. He had never been around a dying man.

"You play it now, Doc," Ike said.

Now?

The old man shut his eyes. Doc sat in the wooden chair next to the bed until Ike snored. Then he tiptoed across the floor, pulling the door partly shut behind him.

Ike was dead a week later.

When Doc went to the house, Ike's wife pushed the screen door open and motioned to him to come inside.

"He passed this morning." Her voice was a soft moan.

"I'm sorry."

"He's in a better place." She smiled. Her lips quivered.

Doc looked at her face. Her eyes were big behind her spectacles. Her gray hair was pulled into a tight bun. She wore a flowered dress that was like all of her other dresses. Doc wondered what memories were playing back in her head right now. He tried to imagine her young, with a full figure and face, in a white Sunday dress, walking with her arm in Ike's on the way to church, maybe going to the club with him on a Friday night; sitting in the front row and proudly listening to her man and his guitar, turning down men seeking a dance, explaining to them simply: "I got my man, thanks."

"I got something on the stove." The house smelled like it always had, moist, starchy, a lingering air of perfume and kitchen spices. She stood in the middle of the living room. She looked toward Ike's guitar case, which stood against the end of the couch.

"He wanted you to have that."

"His guitar?"

She nodded.

He picked up the guitar case. The handle was worn. The rows of brass rivets holding the case together were tarnished.

"Take it home," she said. "He said to tell you that you can play it now."

Doc nodded.

"Thanks."

"Don't thank me. It was him. Just remember him."

Headlights beamed into the motel window, then shut off. An engine shuddered still. Doc peeked through a crack in the curtains and watched a man and a woman get out of the car. She giggled and leaned against him. They went into the room next door.

"This gig is getting to be real work." Doc spoke out loud to the empty motel room.

Sandy had screamed like his mother, a long time ago, when she came home late from a bad date and he had asked her for some money to buy a new guitar.

"Me, me, goddam me, that's all I get out of you." She glared like she hated him, like he and not his old man was the one who had walked out on her. She tossed back her head and swallowed booze mixed with a couple of pills. "You've got more of that son of a bitch in you than you got of me. You're gonna grow up and

118

take that guitar and leave me here alone, you. You. Oh, please."
And the tears came like a sudden rain as she sat at the kitchen
table clutching her glass of liquor and sobbing into her right hand,
then reaching out for him, grabbing him by the shoulder, pulling
him to her, holding him close, crying into his chest. She looked up
at him, the skin around her eyes creased and smudged with damp
eyeliner, her hair thick and crusty with hair spray. He pulled back
from her grasp and she let go with another barrage.

"Go. Run up to your goddam roof, strum your goddam
guitar. You're him all over again. You've had your chance, there
won't be any more hugs from me. Now get out of here."

Doc pulled his clothes off and climbed beneath the sheet and
blankets. He pulled his knees toward his waist and curled into a
warm ball.

Then he sat up. A teardrop glistened in the dark motel room.
Doc's voice spoke in a low, weary moan. "Daddy. Why? Why?"

He closed his eyes to the dim light that pushed through the
cracks of the drapes. He shut his ears to the muffled laughter in the
next room, the distant whir of traffic. He burrowed into the bed
and slept.

VIII

The new guitar pulled on Doc's neck and shoulders like a leaden harness. He struggled to lift his legs, to step forward or backward. It was like trying to move in a deep pool of water.

He formed a G bar chord and pulled the pick across the strings.

The chord screeched, filled with dissonance. Doc's fingers dripped blood onto the floor.

The drummer thumped a rapid, erratic beat on the bass. The backup musicians smirked as Doc wavered between rhythm and lead. He dropped the guitar and let it dangle from his neck.

The instrument had felt ideal in the music store. It had balance. Its shape was comfortable in his hands. It was light.

But now, its neck was fat in his left hand. The strings were too high off the frets. The spacing between them was too tight.

The drummer rapped out another series of random knockings.

None of it was working.

Doc held his bleeding fingers to his face and closed his eyes, then blinked them open as the drummer continued to beat incessantly, incoherently, on the bass.

Ike sat in the front row. He frowned as Doc floundered in mid-chord.

Next to the old man, Sandy laughed as Doc's fingers froze.

All that was left was the beating of the drum, like heavy footsteps plodding through the stillness of sleep.

He opened his eyes into blackness, looked around the room and located the soft glow of the drapes over the window. Someone was knocking at his door.

"Just a minute." He set his legs on the floor, found his pants and pulled them on. He peeked out the fisheye hole into the walkway. A wide, warped face with dark lips looked back at him. He recognized the face and unlocked the door.

"Doc?"

"Uh huh."

Her dark brown hair curled over her shoulders. Her skin was light and clear, almost transparent. Her face was long and thin, her lips red without lipstick.

"Geezus," Doc said.

She stood on the walkway while Doc stared. Their eyes met like they had earlier, when she had danced in front of the stage at the show.

She dropped her eyes to the floor. "I was at your show tonight."

"I know." Doc stepped back from the doorway. "You're the dancing lady."

She smiled and came into the room.

"What time is it?"

"I don't know," she said. "It's late."

Her voice was like butter on toast, damp and soft and warm.

"I thought you'd be awake."

Doc grinned. "No. I eat, I walk and talk. And I sleep."

He stepped back and studied her.

She posed.

"What do you want?"

She sighed and looked into him. "To know you a little bit?"

She wore her concert outfit, a floor-length, thin red skirt and a white blouse with a spray of red roses on it.

Doc motioned to the bed. She pushed the door shut. He reached behind her and pulled it back open. "Have a seat," he said. "I think I'll put on a shirt."

She did a twirl as she glided to the bed. "It's a beautiful night out," she said. "So warm."

"I think you mean a beautiful morning out." Doc grabbed a shirt and went into the bathroom. He looked in the mirror while he buttoned his shirt. He combed his fingers through his hair.

It had been a tough night. Guitarists frequently have to install new strings during a gig. But not new guitars. Especially new guitars after the one you'd replaced had been your instrument for more than three decades, had become part of your body and spirit.

Doc knew every crevice and bend and nick of that old guitar like a husband and wife of 50 years can reach out in the middle of the night and know exactly where the other one is, where to lay the hand so it settles right in the warm spot between the stomach and the thigh.

He peeked around the corner of the bathroom. She was still on the bed. "Just a minute," he said.

"Don't worry. I've got all night."

She had emerged out of the crowd near the end of the second show. She stood in an aisle between tables in front of the stage. The spotlight shone behind her, so Doc could see the outline of her hips swaying beneath her skirt.

He plucked the G string. It vibrated along the neck of the guitar. The woman danced slowly, thrusting her hips forward and backward. He splashed riffs of tremolo blues onto the audience like an artist throws color onto a canvas. The music fell in a soft, misty rain onto the room, gathering like bits of dew in her dark hair that hung to her shoulders and tumbled down her sides and back.

She stared into Doc, her arms out to her side, her head nodding in time to the easy rhythm. She danced with the slow, sad, gonna-bring-it-on-home-to-you-babe-blues Doc played for her. He didn't hear the whoops that echoed his harmonica-like screeches, the oh-baby moans evoked by his slides and bends. He sent his notes directly at her moving target, caressing her with his guitar.

Doc couldn't make her out cleanly in the fuzzy brightness of the room until she stood still, between songs, her eyes boring into him so that he could feel her reading his insides. He looked down at his strings, found a bar chord and strummed it to set up the next tune. When he looked back up there was a blank space where she'd been.

Doc came out of the bathroom. She smiled at him.

"Bet you think I'm a groupie."

Doc shrugged his shoulders.

"Well I'm not."

"Sure. Okay."

When a beautiful woman comes knocking on your door in the middle of the night, you don't argue much. Unless she's selling something.

"I don't have but a few bucks," Doc said.

122

"You wanna go down to the river?"

"Okay."

"I love the river at night."

They went outside. It felt like early morning. The air was still and heavy, the sky black beyond the thin spray of light from the motel.

"I'm parked over here."

They stopped under a yellow spotlight. She looked up into his face. Doc suddenly realized how short she was. And young.

"How old are you?" Doc said.

"How old are you?"

"Okay. That's fair." It had been a long time since a groupie, at least a young one, had come on to Doc. Older women, half drunk, their faces smeared with makeup, had approached him in the clubs he'd played. And there was Vicki. But she was no groupie. She was just a regular woman who happened into his bar one night. A regular woman, whatever that meant, who was lonely like Doc.

"I'm old enough to have a daughter your age," Doc said.

"Do you?"

He shook his head.

"I'm of age. I'm old enough to have bought the bottle I've got in the car."

They climbed into the faded, dark sedan. She turned the ignition key. The exhaust pipe spit a puff of white smoke into the air. She revved the engine a couple of times, then leaned over and opened the glove box. She pulled out a bottle and handed it to Doc.

He unscrewed the lid and took a long gulp, then passed the bottle to her. She turned her head toward him, flashed a bright smile like a flashbulb popping. She threw her head back and drank.

The moon shone dimly through a sheet of clouds that blew across the wide expanse of sky like billowy tumbleweeds. The dream stayed with Doc, the atonal crash of guitar chords repeating itself like a bad song that plays over and over in the mind, the new electric instrument heavy and plodding, his fingers missing their target. The show itself hadn't gone that badly; he'd managed to play some perfunctory solos, to pry some workmanlike licks out of the thing. But this whole gig, this entire traveling blues road show, had gone sour.

"This is strange," Doc said.

She pushed the gear shift into first. The gears gnashed and the car lurched out of the parking lot.

"It's been a long time," Doc said. "I mean, I've been around. I've been with women. But this is different, this here goin' on tonight. I feel like I'm in a dream, except I'm awake. I know that."

She smiled again. She had one of the best smiles Doc had ever seen. It was a loud smile that almost laughed.

"You're with me," she said. "That's different."

"I guess. Yeah."

Doc took another swig of booze. It was cheap whiskey. They drove through the residential district of Albuquerque's north valley, past beige and brown adobe style houses with small porches lit up by yellow porch lights. The city slumbered. The stillness reminded Doc of when his father had driven them out of town a couple of hours before dawn, going to the mountains to go fishing.

Doc and the woman rode through the blackest hour of the night, on the dark side of the thin hem of grayness that becomes a new day.

"What's your name?"

"Tanya."

Her hair hung in waves down the side of her head, shielding her face. Her nose poked out, thin and round at the end. She drove toward the river, rounding the curves of the black two-lane road that meandered through the small rural acreages.

A pair of cat eyes sparkled in the headlights, then blinked off.

It had been a long time since Doc had really seen the night. He had been out in it, drank in it, played cards in it, made music in it. He had been a night person all his life. But not since he was a boy on the roof had he gone out and looked at it, studied it, felt it.

She came to a dirt road that led down into a clump of trees and bushes beneath the steel and concrete bridge that spanned the Rio Grande. Tanya shifted down and steered the car toward the river. The road led into an open parking area, and then disappeared into the woods. She drove to the edge of the river, into the moonshadow of a tall cottonwood, let the engine idle for a few moments, then shut it off. They listened to the stillness.

"C'mon." Tanya opened her door. The dome light flashed on. They went to the front of the car. Tanya hiked up her skirt and pulled herself up onto the hood. Doc sat next to her. The black, wide river flowed slowly past them. Small waves kissed the bank, the water slushing against the eternal mud.

"I come here to be alone sometimes," Tanya said. She looked at Doc. Her eyes were big and white, with black, clear islands in the middle.

"It's nice," Doc said.

They leaned back on their elbows and watched the river. Scraps of light, bits of moon and stars, floated on the water. Animals rustled in the bushes.

"How did you get here?" Doc said.

"To Albuquerque?"

"Yeah. That. And here. This place at this point in time. Did you grow up somewhere? Go to school?"

Tanya sighed. "I'm an Air Force brat. My dad was assigned here when I was a freshman in high school. Before that, it was California. Before that, Texas. Before that, Germany. I'd never lived anywhere longer than three years. The last time, I decided wherever we ended up, I was staying. It was here. He got reassigned again my junior year. I talked my parents into letting me live with a friend and finish high school here. That was almost ten years ago. He's retired now, lives in Yuma Arizona with a fat government pension and he's bringing in another pretty good check selling real estate."

"Life on the road," Doc said. "I've been there."

"As a kid?"

"No. As a musician."

"It's different when you do it by choice."

"It wasn't really by choice. I had to get out of town."

"What, the law?"

Doc laughed. "No. For my sanity. I got burned. I fell, hard, for a woman."

125

"How old were you?"

"A kid. Twenty-four. Twenty-five. I was playin' clubs around town, you know, building a rep. She comes in one night, she's by herself, and she sits at a front table and orders a drink. You know, this was a while ago, before women went out and drank by themselves. But she did. She sat there through two sets and listened to the music. I mean she really listened."

Doc looked out at the river. "She was still there at the end of the night. I'd watched her. These guys would ask her to dance, but she turned 'em down. Just sat there nursing her drink. I still remember, she drank White Russians. The first time I kissed her was that night. I could taste the drink on her."

"Sounds like she's still with you." Tanya put her hand on Doc's leg.

Doc looked at her. "I don't know how to define love. I mean, I'm living with a woman now that I like a whole lot. Y'know? It's not this mad passionate thing where we can't tear ourselves away from each other. But I don't like being without her. With Elise, though, it was like nothing I'd ever felt before. It was the most exciting feeling I'd ever had for another person, not being able to wait until the next day comes so you can see her again, thinking about her every minute you're awake, seeing her face in every crowd you pass through. That first night, when my last set ended, she was still there. The lights came on, I went and sat down to talk to her. You know, I was expecting the usual groupie bullshit – you play good, I like your style crap. But she didn't do that. She started talking about herself, about how she'd been home reading a book listening to the radio and she suddenly felt like getting out and hearing some music. I mean, she explained to me why she had come out, she told me about the book she was reading. For the first time I could remember, I spent the night listening to someone else talk about themselves and their plans. She was so sure of herself, so excited about what she was going to do with her life. She was on a rush, and she caught me up in it. She was going to be on the stage, y'know? That was what she said we had in common. We were both performers. We were showoffs. She used to laugh about that, make fun of how we needed to get up in front of an audience and put on a show. She

126

didn't fill my head with a bunch of crap about how good I was, which was the kind of noise I got from the groupies. I mean, she thought I was a good guitar man, but when she said it, it wasn't bullshit."

"You are, you know," Tanya said.

"Are what?"

"Good."

"C'mon."

They laughed.

"Not tonight, I wasn't," Doc said. "I'm gettin' to know a new guitar, and we didn't hit if off so well."

She leaned her head into the warmth between his shoulder and neck. They listened to the river.

"So what happened to her?"

"We got married about three months later."

Tanya shook her head slowly. "I think I know the rest of the story."

"Just like the song." Doc rested his arms on his legs. Water rippled by, carrying silt and twigs and microscopic solar systems and galaxies of minuscule life to the Gulf of Mexico and the endless, wet, deep ocean.

"I came home one day. You know, a couple hours before she expected me. She was with my drummer." Doc sighed. "My drummer."

"Why do you say it that way? What was wrong with the drummer?"

"Nothing was wrong with him. He was just a dumb shit. A boring dumb shit, that's all. I never could figure what she saw in him; she was so flighty, so spur-of-the-moment. He was plain dull. I mean, he was good looking, with this curly hair and a pretty face, almost like a girl. But that was it. There was nothing to him. He went through life boom-chick-a-boom, laying down rhythms behind everyone else, banging out a beat."

"So what happened?"

"I turned around and walked out. I found the closest bar. I sat there with a single shot of whiskey that I sipped on for a couple of hours. For the first time in my life I nursed a drink. Then I went back home at the time I was supposed to be there. She was gone."

"You mean, gone? For good?"

"Yeah. She didn't leave a note or anything."

"Did you guys fight?"

"Sure. We fought. We screwed. We did everything married people do. Except stay married. But I guess most married people do that too, get unmarried."

"Did you ever see her again?"

"No. I left town. Went on the road. I heard about the drummer, though. He dropped her and went to Nashville. Get that, man. He dropped her."

"And he made it big in Nashville."

Doc scratched his head and smirked. "Nope. Last I heard, he was tending bar at some honky-tonk." Doc shook his head. "Pullin' beers for everybody else. He was always a back-seat guy."

"And you went on the road."

Yeah. A two-year road trip, the Doctor Blues traveling music show. Hank Sweeny on bass. Merle Thompson on piano. And the drummer, Timekeeper Will, a black kid who swayed his bald head in time to the high hat. They lived out of a panel truck, stayed in motels on the edge of town that always had the vacant sign up, hitting small-town bars for weekend jobs, something to bring in the rubes and liven up their lives with a dance and a blues.

The river bumped against the bank. There's a time of day, somewhere in the middle of midnight and dawn, you can feel a change in the air. Doc had felt it as a boy, camping with his father, he'd wake up and hear his father breathing next to him. A breeze comes up, there's a rustle in the air, and then you hear the river move. Something to do with the sun heading your way, passing some orbital point that clicks your part of the world away from yesterday and into tomorrow, a span of a millisecond when time shifts. The river bubbles, sighs, and it flows a little louder for a moment.

Two years on the road gathered in Doc's memory like a series of snapshots: one-night stands with country women who wandered into the nightclub off a rural road, looking to make time with a traveling minstrel, to touch a piece of the bigger world beyond the gates of town; breakfasts of hash and eggs and bacon cooked within one shade of brown away from burnt; waitresses who propped their legs on counter stools and yakked while you drank coffee and tried to figure out which direction was best to find a club owner willing to pay you and booze you for a weekend's worth of music; hot summer nights with a sweating six-pack of beer and a deck of cards and all the clubs are closed because you're in a blue county that doesn't allow any liquor or dancing because it's a Sunday, God's night off; eternal strips of black highway that roll into the horizon, billboards promising gas and salvation in the next town; splitting two cans of pork and beans and one apple four ways because the promised gig was given to another band that played for cheaper wages; barrooms with faded paint and neon beer signs, whiskered men and frumpy women filling in the same stools and tables, laughing and smoking and drinking to forget their work and their impending deaths for one more night; Hank and Merle and Timekeeper gathered on a small wooden stage, and for one night, the four of them play a blues like it's never been played, their instruments meshing like the polished gears of an atomic clock, they trade solos and fill gaps with gritty chords of blues, and Doc will never forget the night he played the almost perfect blues riff that was slow and fast, and each finger landed directly on key except for the notes where he hovered just above the flat and bent the note smoothly into the neighborhood of the next one, and when the song was over, the musicians stopped for a minute, smiled at each other, took a drink and enjoyed the taste of a well-played song. This is why you do it.

Tanya nuzzled into Doc's neck. She stood between him and the river. Doc could hear her breath, her heart. He heard when she swallowed. He pulled back and looked into her face. It caught the moonlight. Her eyes sparkled. Most of her life was still in front of her.

"What are you doing out here in the middle of the night with a beat up old guitar player?"

She shrugged and smiled. Her teeth lined up in a neat row. "When you're a kid who moves around a lot, you learn to enjoy life one day at a time, and that's what I'm doing. I like the kind of music you play, and when I watched you on the stage tonight, I saw the way you looked at me. I felt the same way."

"Lonely?"

She nodded.

"I'll never understand how a good-looking woman – and there is no other kind – can be lonely. Ever."

"It happens. A lot."

Doc held her. He wrapped his arms around her and petted her hair, stroked her back. She breathed into him, and he could feel her breasts against his stomach. He felt her fingers on his spine. He closed his eyes and remembered holding Elise, when he was young, and he didn't know it was important to hold her and to savor holding her and to sear into his memory the smell of her, the way she walked, how she folded into him when they slept naked in the summertime with the sheets and blankets off. Then life was forever and he knew it always would be.

"You want to go back to the room?"

Tanya nodded. "I'm starting to get chilly."

On the way downtown, Doc sipped Tanya's whiskey, and he anticipated her. He watched her as she drove, her eyes on the road, her hands sure on the steering wheel, the pre-dawn gray breeze blowing through her open window, tossing the strings of her hair across her face.

In the motel room, they undressed in the dark. They pulled a sheet around themselves and then, as they caressed each other, Doc reached across her and turned on the lamp next to the bed.

"What are you doing?"

Doc propped himself on the pillow and stared at Tanya's body. Her hair curled down over her breasts. Her belly was a soft, round mound of light brown flesh.

"I'm looking at you."

"I'm just a woman, like any other."

"I know. It's been a long time for me, Tanya."

She turned off the light and pulled Doc into her.

In the morning, Doc awoke with his arm around Tanya. The room was bright. He lay on his side, listening to her breathe, wondering what she was dreaming. The back of her body was warm against him. Her hair went in a hundred directions. Doc pressed his nose into her neck and smelled her. She was different than Elise. Than Vicki. Than the women he had slept with on the

130

road, the women he had drunk with in the clubs until he was full of booze and tired and ready to make blind love and fall into a dizzy, exhausted sleep. She was all of them.

"Your nose is cold."

Doc pulled back. "Sorry."

Tanya giggled. "That's okay." She turned over and faced the ceiling.

"What time is it?"

"I don't know," Doc said. "I quit wearing a watch years ago. Does it matter?"

"No." She looked at him. "You any good in the morning?"

She brushed her leg against Doc's. Her hand went between his thighs, and she gently caressed him. Doc slipped his arm under her and rolled her onto him. They made love as the morning traffic buzzed outside and traveling businessmen made appointments and discussed deals in the motel parking lot.

Afterwards, Tanya sat on the side of the bed, her back to Doc. She took a brush from her purse and pulled it through her hair. She shook her hair loose and tied it behind her like a thick horse's tail.

"Mind if I use your toothbrush?"

Doc leaned against a pile of pillows, the blankets pulled up over his chest, and he watched Tanya wash herself and do her teeth.

They walked to the diner on the corner. Bacon fried on the grill. A man in checkered pants and white shirt painted melted, yellow butter onto slices of toast.

Doc ordered steak and eggs with a side of hash browns. Tanya got a hot cinnamon roll and coffee.

"Where you going next?" Tanya sipped the coffee. Puffs of steam rose out of the brown mug.

"Just down the road." Doc dipped toast into an egg yolk. "El Paso. After that, I don't know. My road manager handles all that stuff."

"How long will you be on tour?"

"I don't know. That's the strange thing about this whole deal. Every three or four days, Sandy, that's my road manager, she gets instructions from Dex, he's the guy runnin' this show near as

I can tell. He books the acts and makes all the arrangements, and then she takes care of things at this end. She tells me tickets are getting harder to sell lately. The other day she said the tour's about over. I don't know. It's some kind of numbers game."

"Everything's a numbers game." Tanya motioned to the counterman for more coffee.

"Tell me. Yeah. This whole concert gig is based on some kind of computer projections. Everything's all planned out. Before each show, Sandy tells me which one of two sets I'm supposed to play, and each set you play the same songs in the same order. It's all scientific. There's no room for me to do anything different."

"But the show's making money, right? The one I was at last night was sold out."

"I guess. Sandy and Dex handle all the money. They give me a weekly allowance, and I'm supposed to get a percentage when the whole thing's over. Sometimes I feel like I'm a goddam hooker, y'know?"

Doc mopped up egg yolk with his toast. The diner was full. Men wearing plaid shirts and cowboy hats and blue jeans and captain's hats and work denims lined the counter, sipping coffee, thumbing through the newspaper, smoking cigarettes. At the end of the counter, a waitress poured fresh coffee into a mug while she fanned her eyebrows at her customer and grinned through orange lipstick at the story he told. A couple of families filled the booths along the far wall, and groups of men and women sat at the island of booths and tables in the middle of the diner. A bell hooked up to the front door jangled whenever anybody went out or came in. The place was a morning version of a nightclub. The loners, lined up along the counter drinking coffee, were like the singles who parked at the club bar. These were the ones who came every day, the hardcore, habitual diner crowd. Out on the floor, the more occasional customers and the one-stops mingled in groups. The women behind the counter, the man at the grill, the cashier who stood behind the register by the front door, these were the morning versions of the bartenders and barmaids and doormen. These were the order keepers, the providers.

The only thing missing was the booze and the cover of night. Otherwise, the morning diner and midnight blues club were the photograph and the negative of a universal scene: people gathering together in a communal sharing of eating, drinking and conviviality.

Doc finished his coffee. He laid his napkin on the table and leaned back against the booth cushion. "When I was young, you worked clubs and built up a name, then when you got a rep you might be an opener for some big name coming to town, you sort of worked your way up a ladder. Some people went all the way up. They were lucky, y'know? Or they had connections. It had absolutely nothing to do with talent, believe me. Very little, anyway. Others found their own level and sort of stayed there. The man I learned from, he played in one town his whole life. But you couldn't go into that town without hearing his name. It was his town. When a traveling band came in for a gig, it was his club they went to after hours. Man, he did it right."

Doc caught himself. "I sound like an old man, don't I? Talking about how things used to be, when I was young. Man, don't let me bore you."

Tanya rubbed her foot against Doc's leg under the table.

"You're no old man. Anyway, you weren't an old man last night. Or this morning." She smiled.

Doc felt himself blush.

"Any chance you might ever get back this way?"

Doc shrugged. "We haven't repeated any towns yet."

"So I guess I'll probably never see you again."

"I guess."

"That's too bad. I like you, Doc."

"I like you, too."

Tanya took a pencil and paper from her purse. She wrote her name and number and handed it to Doc. "Just in case. You ever find yourself back here, give me a call."

Doc folded the paper and slipped it into his shirt pocket. He watched Tanya as she dabbed her lips with a napkin. She took a mirror from her purse and looked into it.

Doc wondered what she saw in there, if she saw a beautiful young woman with a life ahead of her, if she saw a woman with time running out and no man and no children in sight. He wondered if she saw anything beyond tonight and maybe tomorrow morning. He studied her eyes, which were a dark brown in the morning light, as she patted her hair into place and snapped her compact shut. He realized he didn't know much about her.

"I wish I was going to be here longer," he said. "I'd like to know you better."

"So when your concert's over, stop back when you're on your way to wherever. Stay awhile. God knows this town could use a good blues band."

Doc nodded. He patted his shirt pocket. "I'll save this number."

Tanya stood up. "I gotta go."

Doc wondered where she had to be in the morning. After so many years, you stop asking people those kinds of questions.

Suddenly he wanted to know more about her.

Tanya leaned over and gave Doc a kiss on the cheek. "I had a good time," she said into his ear, her breath warm and soft.

Then she was walking toward the door, her hair bouncing against her back, her buttocks swishing back and forth inside her skirt, and Doc was the only one in the place who knew she didn't have anything on underneath.

I had a good time too, Doc thought. He couldn't remember when he had talked so much.

The doorbell tinkled. Tanya walked past the front window and was gone.

IX

The sun shone in a high, cloudless sky as Doc and Sandy followed the Rio Grande Valley south, toward Texas. He sat in the back seat of the van and worked his fingers over and over the frets of his guitar, trying to get a comfortable feel of the thing, to get his hands used to the shape and mood of the instrument. He picked along quietly with the songs on the radio. Warm, dry air blew through the windows. A black speck of a vulture soared high in the sky, its wings sitting on a thermal shelf. Brown scrub brush and dirt whizzed by the open window. Dead insect bodies made tiny Rorschach blots on the windshield.

Doc's eyelids sagged. The tires whirred steadily over the road.

Sandy took a drink from the bottle between her legs. It had been full when she and Doc pulled out of the motel parking lot early in the morning. The bottle was about five shots down by now, the brown booze lapping against the clear glass as the van slid over the pimpled highway.

Doc yawned and fought sleep. It had been two days since he'd slept all night. The bar fight seemed like years ago. His time with Tanya was far away. The whole tour seemed like a long-ago memory, a jumble of one-nighters and two-nighters, motel rooms that all had the same carpeting and walls and color televisions, chromium-framed prints bolted to the walls, white washcloths and towels, windows with thick white drapes that somehow held the light from outside like an eternal, wall-length night light. The concerts were an endless chord exercise, with a few different solo licks tossed in like a dash of salt added to an omelet, enough to flavor the thing a little differently from the same dish served in another city three nights before.

Sandy tapped her thumbs on the steering wheel in time to the music on the radio, and she mouthed the words of the song to herself. She held the van in a straight line on the dark pink road.

Her only words to Doc since the bar fight and the parking lot scene had been to tell him which set to play the night before – the

135

Tanya night, the glorious gap in the long-play tape this tour had become.

He felt in his pocket and found the slip of paper with Tanya's phone number. Tanya had reminded him of Elise.

Vicki came close. He was comfortable with Vicki. She was somebody he could easily spend morning and night with. He relaxed with Vicki, liked to watch her when she curled in the couch with the television on, which she ignored while she read a book. He enjoyed their Sunday mornings cooking breakfast together. Sundays were his and Vicki's shared break from the world, the end of his work week, of the bars filled with chatter and laughter and smoke, the day before her return to the sterile nurse's station where she wore her crisp uniforms and her sparkling eyeglasses and kept track of patients and pills and doctors' rounds.

Vicki planned things out. She could sit in one place for an hour doing one thing. She worked for others and cheerfully did what her bosses told her to do. But Elise and Tanya – he could tell this even after just one night – were a different kind of woman. They set their own agendas, which usually consisted of whatever they felt like doing just now. Once, he and Elise had driven to the mountains. Spring was merging into summer. The days were hot. The nights were almost frigid. They had found a stream, and without even a look his way, Elise stripped her clothing off and was chest deep, sitting in a black pool of water in the shade of a boulder, eyeing him with a look that said she didn't give a damn if he approved or if he joined her, but what a good time they could have if he got undressed and came in.

Another time, as they drove to an after-hours club on a Friday night, the car radio was blaring and the song reminded Doc of a trumpet man who had suddenly lost his lip at a jam session the week before – with a little help. Doc and the bassist had spiked the man's drink with lemon juice, a little payback for all the times the trumpeter had stepped on their solos. When his turn rolled around, the trumpet man took a sip of his drink, blew into the mouthpiece, and all that came out was the blast of a loud, throaty fart.

Doc and Elise laughed at the story. Then Doc looked across the seat and saw tears glistening in her eyes. She looked over at him with a wide frown, then turned her head to the window and wiped away the tears.

"What's the matter? Why you cryin'?"

"Nothing. Please. Nothing."

He touched her knee. She grasped his hand and held it.

"It's just this, all this," she said. "I'm happy. And I know it's not going to last. It never has."

Doc pulled the car into an alley, and he held Elise. He kissed her cheeks and tasted the salty tears. "We can do whatever we want to," he said. "We can make it last or not."

"I know. Logically, I know that. But it never does."

"Watch. We are in control of our lives. I'll show you we can do whatever we want whenever we want. I don't want to go to the jam tonight. I want to go home with you instead. Now watch."

Doc drove the car out of the alley and toward home. They went into the house. Without speaking, they undressed and got under the blankets. Doc caressed her and kissed her and held her until the sun came up, and they slept through the morning wrapped into each other.

After one night, Doc knew that Tanya was the same. Capable of improvisational bursts of laughter, impulsive lovemaking, and then a half hour later she sat with her knees pulled up to her face, daydreaming about another time, another place. Or another man. Either of these women could love one man one hour and another man the next, without a twinge of guilt.

How? Why?

Doc slowly shook his head as the van rounded the Franklin Mountains and headed into El Paso. What is it about the free spirit that prohibits it from settling into life, from contentment, from goddam honest loyalty?

Sandy cackled laughter. She peered straight ahead through her sunglasses, the smirk on her face the sole remnant of her secret inner amusement. Now here, Doc thought, was a woman who could be relied on for a drink and a good time. And – the standard lament of the country and blues standards – he hadn't wanted her. Doc mouthed a blues tune to himself: Ain't it always the way that ya don't love the one ya got.

137

Downtown El Paso poked its skyscrapers into a light brown smog. Heat waves rose off the pavement of the highway. Doc had overheard Sandy talking to Dexter on the phone earlier. The show was half sold. A radio station promo had filled about another 200 seats. That meant Sandy would be boozing with some disc jockey after the show, then heading to his place or taking him to her motel room. And Doc would end up in another lounge watching all the lonely drinkers ponder their memories and regrets and excuses.

This gig really wasn't much different than a factory job anymore. Except that he didn't get benefits, and there was nobody around to grab a beer with after work. There were no jam sessions like at The Century Sky Room, where all the musicians knew each other and the customers were regulars and you could hang out and not even play if you didn't feel like it.

Sandy took a downtown exit. The city was brown and dusty. The yellow lawns on the fringe of town struggled out of the crusty sod, where the unyielding summer sun sat on them like a blanket. Fat women with shiny black hair strode slowly along the sidewalks, carrying shopping bags and purses that hung limp and heavy from thick shoulder straps.

Downtown, Sandy circled the plaza, where old men and women with furrowed faces sat on wire and wood benches under short, thirsty trees that threw glimpses of shade onto the sparse lawn. Women with children, in town to shop for diapers and frocks and 99-cent plastic toys, gathered in the shady recesses, where boom boxes shouted salsa music and top-40 rock 'n' roll. Sooty buses girded the square like an Old West wagon train pulled into a circle. Their engines rattled while their exhaust pipes spit brown fumes onto the cement street.

Sandy sat at a red light and sipped whiskey as she watched the downtown scene, the streets crowded with workers, men in thick black moustaches that curled around their lips, women who wore scarves over their long, dark hair. Rich Mexicans from across the border, in town for a day of American shopping, strolled the sidewalks. American cars waited in line to cross the muddy Rio Grande into Mexico to stock up on cheap cigarettes and tequila. In the middle of it all, an amateur preacher pranced about on a square of cement, his harangue just a decibel above the daytime downtown din.

"Jesus is in me and he's in you. He's in all of us, if we only open the doors of our hearts and say, come in Jesus, I want you in my life. I love you, Jesus. Save me."

"Brother." Sandy swallowed a mouthful of booze. She poked her head out the window to check for traffic, pulled into the turn lane and drove away from the heart of town.

Old and New Mexico blended in the downtown neighborhoods on the northern fringes of the city. High-rise office towers and banks stood over pawn shops and clothing-by-the-rack and bargain furniture outlets. Rectangular brick apartment houses, turn-of-the-century stone buildings with cracks like varicose veins along the lines of their foundations, cinder brick hovels where children in white underwear played with red tricycles and wagons with wheels that squeaked endlessly along with the locusts in the afternoon heat gave way to modern stucco homes with stone and cactus landscaping and clean, red tile roofs. To the south, sitting in the cloud of smog, was ancient Ciudad Juarez, Mexico, with its neighborhoods of cardboard and pine shacks, its rows of shops pandering to American dollars, its black-haired boys seeking their day's wages in selling trinkets to American tourists, its cool, dark bars offering cheap Mexican and American beers.

Sandy found a motel at the base of the jagged hills that form the Franklin Mountains, a lower appendage of the Rocky Mountains that splits El Paso into two. She waited quietly, popping a wad of chewing gum in her mouth while Doc unloaded his guitars and traveling bags. In the lobby, she took care of the room arrangement at the desk. Doc stood beneath a vent that blew cool air down into the room. Sandy handed him a room key. "We got a sound check and rehearsal in about an hour," she said. "I'll meet you here."

Doc nodded and watched as she carried her bags outside and down the sidewalk. He stepped back into the sun-shiny afternoon. The white cement of the sidewalk radiated heat into the air. In his room, Doc put in a wake-up call for one hour, kicked off his shoes and lay down on top of the blankets. The steady hum of the air conditioner lulled him to sleep.

139

The sound check and rehearsal went quickly. The back-up band was solid, an electric bass, organist and a small, brown drummer who didn't speak English but who played a clean, smooth shuffle and knew how to listen. Doc nodded his approval as they brought a Chicago blues riff to a close. He looked out at the house, the rows of empty seats that tonight would be filled with drunken blues fans passing flasks of booze and joints up and down the aisles, whooping at the music, demanding louder, faster music, applauding lead licks and slow, wavering chord extensions.

"Sounds good," Sandy said. She stood next to Doc, peering out over the empty auditorium.

"We sold out?"

"The house'll be full," she said. "Listen. How about I buy you a drink?"

"What's the occasion?"

"No occasion." She looked into Doc's face. "I'm sure you've figured out by now this thing's coming to an end. I just want to get a drink and talk things over, that's all."

Doc nodded. "I've never turned down a free drink in my life. No reason to start now."

They went outside. The late afternoon heat sat on the city. Sandy drove the van a few blocks toward town, then turned off into the parking lot of a neighborhood beer house on the edge of downtown. They walked into the dark tavern and found a booth with wooden benches across from the bar. A couple of men in cowboy hats played pool in the back room. A cigarette smoldered on the bank, sending a lazy plume of white smoke up into the neon light.

Sandy ordered a shot and beer for Doc and a glass of whiskey for herself.

"You always pick such nice clubs for your drinking." Doc smiled.

"You should be used to this kind of place."

"Hey. I was kidding around. Don't take everything so personal."

Sandy grinned. "I guess I do have kind of a thin skin. But I'm not used to buying drinks for men who say no to me."

140

"Geezus, Sandy. Is that still botherin' you? Aren't men ever allowed to not be in the mood?"

"That wasn't it and you know it." Sandy drank her whiskey like a 50-year veteran of hard-luck bars. Doc kept up with her.

"But it doesn't matter," Sandy said. "Tonight's the last show. We'll pay you off and you can go your own way."

"Fine," Doc said. "I've been gettin' kind of homesick lately."

"Home? I had a feeling you might be headin' back to Albuquerque."

"Albuquerque? Why?"

"I hear you met a nice girl up there."

The bartender brought another set of drinks to the booth. The men in the back laughed as pool balls clicked together.

"How much money I got coming?" Doc said.

"Back to business? Okay." Sandy opened her purse and took out a black notebook. She skimmed a couple of pages. Doc finished off his second beer and whiskey and held up two fingers to the bartender.

"Dex told me you have nine thousand dollars coming. Then he said to deduct the expenses you agreed to in the contract."

Doc felt for his wallet, then remembered. He had folded the contract and put it in his wallet that night in the bar with Dexter, then had thrown it in Vicki's desk. He'd never sat down and studied the thing.

"You know as well as I do what's in the contract," Sandy said. "I've been keeping a tab. You get part of the house and CD and DVD sales. We deduct clothing, the new guitar. Geez, you cost a lot of liquor."

Doc nodded. "I know. It's my once vice. That, and the way I live." He grinned.

But Sandy was all numbers and contract now. "I figure at the end of the night you got about seven thousand coming. That's rounding things off in your favor."

"Hold on. Hold on. I didn't know I had to pick up my own lodging."

"It's in the contract."

"But Dexter said ... I mean, meals."

141

"All we cover is the pre-concert and on-the-road meals. Not room service and meals while we're off-road. It's in the contract."

Sandy smiled and blinked her eyelashes at him. "Doc, you read the contract, didn't you?"

"Sure. Sure I did."

"Then you know all of this. Look, seven thousand dollars is a lot of money for a man who's used to taking home no more than a couple hundred a week. It's a pretty good stake, Doc, wherever you end up."

That was true. Doc would never have saved that much. This would buy time to reestablish himself, find a steady gig, put together a house band.

It also was true that Doc was being suckered. And he knew there wasn't anything he could do. He'd gone into this thing knowing the pile he was stepping into, and his mind numbed. He shrugged his shoulders and nodded at Sandy.

"I'll have the money for you after tonight's show, Doc."

Doc's mind was in another place already; it was in a small nightclub, where he was playing Doc's blues Doc's way with Doc's band for Doc's audience. Just like Ike's gig. Goddam, Doc thought. It takes a lifetime of learning to figure some things out, like how life ought to be lived.

"We need to head back, Doc," Sandy said. "I want to mention one more expense to you."

"Yeah?" Doc looked up and saw Sandy grinning at him from across the table, running her tongue along her lips to mop up the final substance of any whiskey that might still linger there.

"That fling you had in Albuquerque cost you two hundred dollars. That's a lot of money to pay for a piece of ass. But I had to find out if you had it in you. Tanya. Wasn't that her name? I gave her two hundred bucks to spend the night with you. Was she worth it?"

Doc's face flushed hot. He was glad it was dark in the bar so that Sandy couldn't see his face, his angry eyes.

"Every cent of it," he said calmly.

They stood up. Sandy dropped a dollar on the table. "I'll get the tip, Doc."

In the back room, one of the cowboys snorted laughter. Doc turned around and glared at the sound, watched the two men move around the table and position themselves for the next shot. He relaxed. He listened as they gossiped softly about their wives and lovers and wins and losses.

He tailed Sandy out the door into the warm West Texas evening, with the early stars sparkling dimly in a sky that was edging from dark blue into blackness. He reached into his pocket, found Tanya's phone number and tossed it into the air. A breeze caught the slip of paper and carried it toward Mexico.

"C'mon Doc, you got a show in an hour."

He followed Sandy to the van. She handed him the bottle of whiskey from the glove box. He took a drink and gave it to her. She tilted her head back and took a couple of big gulps.

"Tastes good, don't it Doc?"

Sandy belched and kicked the ignition on. "C'mon, Doc. It's over. Lighten up."

They pulled out of the dusty parking lot and left the small, white bar glowing a soft pink in the sunset.

Doc turned his head and watched the dusky strips of shops and houses and hills out the window. He concentrated on not thinking about anything but the immediate sights of the city. He concentrated on keeping his mouth closed and his thoughts cool. He concentrated on the small things of life about him, the individual notes of the cowboy music on the radio, the taste of the liquor on his tongue and cheeks, all the way to the back door of the arena where he would play his final road gig.

Backstage, a full bottle of Scotch and another of bourbon stood behind a tray of sandwiches and chips. A row of plastic cups was stacked next to a plastic gray tub of ice. The Mexican drummer was pouring a cup half full of coke and topping it with bourbon when Doc came in with his two guitars, the new electric and the acoustic.

"Make one for me, would ya pal?" Doc said.

The drummer shrugged his shoulders. Doc pointed at the drink. The drummer smiled and took a swallow.

"Never mind." Doc leaned his guitars against the wall and went to the small buffet. He filled a cup with ice and poured the brown booze over it. He held it up to the drummer.

"Like that."

The drummer smiled again and sipped his drink.

Doc drank his cup half down, refilled it and then found a chair against the wall. He drank quietly as the musicians and stage hands bustled in and out of the room.

Finally Sandy came in. Her eyes were half red. Her hair hung loose, with strands of it criss-crossing, going its own direction. A couple of wrinkles ran out of the corners of her eyes.

She sighed. "This all the booze we got?"

Nobody answered.

"Well, I got mine." She picked up the Scotch and an empty cup, no ice, and sat down in a corner of the room. Doc and the drummer eyed the bottle of bourbon and headed for the table for refills. Doc held his cup of ice in front of him and the drummer filled it to the top.

"Good." Doc winked. "We'll do fine together."

Sandy and Doc sat on opposite sides of the room and drank their booze. It was close and warm. Beyond the door, a tape of Freddie King blues played through the speaker system. Stage hands – college students picking up a few bucks they'd probably spend later that night on a Juarez binge – carried patch cords and microphones and wires in and out of the room. On stage, somebody hammered the bass drum to the floor. Feedback squealed through the auditorium. A steady buzz of voices and laughter told Doc the place was filling up.

A voice came from the doorway. A man poked his head into the room. "Time for the band." It was the local disc jockey talent. "Hi Sand." The head smiled. Its eye winked at Sandy.

She lifted her cup in a toast to the disc jockey and grinned.

Doc figured she was two, maybe three years away from a steady bar seat in some skid row shot-and-beer dive.

He sipped his bourbon and listened to the band play its warm-up tune, a simple Kansas City shuffle they had put words to, incomprehensible words by the time the music sifted through the curtains and the closed stage door, but probably words having to do with love gone bad. Goddam there are a lot of songs on that subject, so many variations on the same theme. Poems, books, songs, movies, all about the promise of love that nine times out of ten failed somebody and sent them tumbling into the bottles or taking to the road. But that wasn't really what the blues was about. No, the blues was more about living but feeling like you're dying. Or maybe wanting to die. Hell, the blues could even be about wanting to live but not feeling much like you can. Doc grinned. His whole life, all of it he could remember anyway, he'd tried to define this thing he felt, this combination of lonely and desolate, the occasional glee that made the solitary groping that much stronger. It wasn't wanting to die, and it wasn't wanting to live. It was wanting to feel something when you don't and not wanting to feel something when you do. Yeah. Maybe that was it. Wanting. Always wanting.

He laughed out loud.

"What you got over there?" Sandy smiled at him. They were the only two in the room.

"I'm just figuring things out."

"Let me know when you get there, and tell me how it's done."

They stared across the room at each other while the muffled tones of the band seeped through the door.

The disc jockey's head came into the doorway again.

"You're up, Doc."

Doc stood up. A rush of dizziness filled his head, then was gone, like a gust of wind that surprises a calm afternoon and then skips away. He drank his plastic cup empty, then filled it to the brim.

"Play the train set, Doc."

He looked down at Sandy, propped against the wall.

"I think I'll play whatever the hell I feel like playin'."

"Doc," she stared to explain, her words slurring. "I've told you how it works. I figure the crowd; a roomful of couples, they get the love song set. The bawdier crowd, they get the train set. It's all figured out, Doc." She blinked her eyes at him.

"This last night, it's my set. It's what the hell I want to play." Doc carried his cup of whiskey onto the stage. He watched

145

as the band players stood at their instruments, then he walked toward them as the disc jockey announced his name. There was applause somewhere, but it was like noise from another room. The stage was still, almost quiet. The musicians stared at Doc as he moved across the stage. The drummer wore a big smile. Doc found his microphone, and he turned to face the audience.

"Rock 'n' roll," somebody shouted near the front.

"Ow! Get down, Doctor man."

The crowd was a lake of heads moving in choppy waves, bandanas and glowing cigarettes bobbing along the surface. He turned toward the organ player as he strapped on his acoustic.

"Gimme a twelve-bar in E."

The organist nodded. Doc played a simple one-bar four-chord intro and landed on the E chord. He stepped to the mike and sang.

"I've got the key to the highway; I'm packed and ready to go; I'm gonna leave here runnin'; walkin's just too slow."

He finished the first verse and pulled his head back from the mike, moving his fingers glibly up and down the guitar, playing a solo into the microphone placed in front of his belly to pick up the strings.

For three songs, Doc played acoustic blues, Mississippi Delta and Chicago blues. He played the blues he'd learned from Ike – young blues, striving for perfection blues, searching for the chord that's never been played blues. He played Sonny Boy Williamson's "Mighty Long Time" and T-Bone Walker's "Call it Stormy Monday," moving from song to song with a pause for a drink and a breath of dusty, smoke-tinged air in between. He grinned as his fingers hit home, landing as truly on each fret and string as a piano hammer striking the wires inside a gleaming black grand. Doc chuckled and led his fingers on a walk and then a stroll and then an easy run up and down the neck of his guitar, making each song his song, invoking pieces of Ike into each tune, stopping between songs to explain to the audience that "when you've loved a man, or spent time with a woman, that person is going to be in you for the rest of your life, and he, she, they're in these blues I'm playin' for ya."

He took a sip of his drink and set it back on top of the amp. "But that probably don't make no sense to anybody in here but me," he said, looking down into the throat of the microphone as he talked. "Right?" He gave his strings a blind strum.

"Amen, Doc," someone in the middle of the room shouted.

Doc grinned. "Here's one that has a little piece of El Paso in it."

He played "Sittin' on Top of the World." And when he got to the words "up from El Paso; sayin' come back baby, I need you so," the audience whooped and clapped because this foreign musician had come into their town and played a song with their town in its lyric. He ended the tune with the third verse, "And now love's gone, but I don't worry; Because I'm sittin' on top of the world."

He talked into the microphone as he unstrapped the acoustic guitar. "How many of you ever been in love?"

The auditorium responded with whistles and cheers.

"How many of you ever lost your love?"

A woman's voice cried from the back. "Yes, Doc!"

He hooked his electric guitar around his body and pointed toward the woman's voice. "This next one's for you," he said. "And me. Cuz I've lost love, too."

He nodded to the band. "Let's do it in A, guys. Just follow along."

Doc moved up to the tenth fret and picked an electric A out of the guitar. He bent the note twice and let it echo through the room.

The guitar felt good.

"You're alright, Doc!" came from the audience.

Doc grinned and moved his pick up and down, playing grace notes and sixteenths and thirty-seconds around the lead notes, be-bopping in a jazzy style through a fast blues-picking solo. His guitar ached and sobbed and wailed as Doc played a yearning 12-bar love-lost extended blues intro, then finally stepped up to the microphone.

"The thrill is gone," he sang.

The audience let loose with waves of applause and yelps.

147

"The thrill is gone away; the thrill is gone; the thrill is gone away; you know you done me wrong; and you'll be sorry some day."

He stepped back from the mike and rephrased the same solo he'd played entering the song. In front of him, from left to right, the auditorium was full of heads bobbing to the music, glints of eyeglasses, flashes of matches, smiling teeth, blonde hair, black moustaches, beards and ponytails, T-shirts and work shirts, skirts, pants, bare feet. People danced in the aisles. Directly ahead, a round, white spotlight bored through the swimming blackness into Doc's face.

He closed his eyes and played the blues of a lost father. He played the song of a mother who wanders from room to room, dragging a half-empty bottle of liquor behind her as she searches the corners and cupboards for love. He played a tune of long, sleepless summer nights awake in bed and listening to the sounds of a city where people are caught in momentary ecstasy and longing agony. And he played the vacant, forlorn blues of a man who gambled his soul on a woman and came up a loser.

He played some of Doc's blues.

"The thrill is gone; it's gone away from me; the thrill is gone; it's gone away from me. Although I'll still live on; oh so lonely I'll be."

Doc's fingers pulled and pushed and bent the blues of love and hope and loss and despair. He looked to the side of the stage and saw Sandy watching him from behind the curtain.

"The thrill is now; I'm free from your spell; I'm free, free now; I'm free from your spell. And now that it's all over; all I can do is wish you well."

Doc played a final chord, laying it across the room like a cloud, then stepped back from the microphone and stood in the applause like a man in a soothing hot shower after eight hours of sweat labor.

The house was Doc's. He mixed road songs and train songs and love songs. He played fast electric blues and slow folk blues. He played Ike's songs and Doc's songs and Willie Dixon and Robert Johnson and Sonny Terry and Brownie McGhee and T-Bone Walker. He was like a disc jockey fed up with the playlist

148

who pulls every song he ever loved out of the library to play, ignoring commercials, omitting the hits, oblivious to the threat of loss of livelihood and sponsor.

The audience members, on their feet, clapped along, dancing, singing, shouting, relaying flasks and joints up and down the rows until finally the lights came on and the residue of smoke drifted through the place, with the dim yellow ceiling lights stabbing through it. Doc went backstage and soothed his throat with a cup of ice covered with bourbon.

Sandy held a phone to her ear and talked through the clamor of stage hands tearing down the show. Janitors swept the floor, banging trash cans into dumpsters. Hangers-on lolled at the door, peeking in at Doc and the other musicians, shouting congratulations for a good show.

Sandy looked at Doc as she talked on the phone.

He smiled at her.

She turned away.

A little past midnight, the black van pulled into the motel parking lot. Somewhere in a barroom off the street, glasses tinkled, a jukebox blared and voices laughed and gabbed. A big yellow moon hung in the sky. The van door slid open, footsteps padded onto the pavement, and the door slid shut. The van groaned and wheeled away, leaving Doc and his guitars in the middle of the parking lot under a twinkling sky.

He went to his room and laid his guitars on the spare bed. He sat in a chair in front of the window and listened to the soft hum just beyond the door. He wet his throat with warm whiskey and tried to figure out the source of the buzzing: a light bulb, a drink machine, the neon sign that glowed in the desert night announcing rooms and cable TV and free local calls. Or maybe it was an electronic cicada. There's no telling anymore what a noise might be.

The night crawled by, broken up by the whir of traffic out on the road, the ghostly passings of car radios singing songs and selling tires and predicting a high of 95 with overnight lows in the upper 70s. Women giggled on the parking lot, men talked in low voices, room lights clicked on, beer cans popped open. Someone scooped a bucket of ice from the machine that whirred and clicked

149

every minute, dropping cold, clear teardrops onto a hill of frozen cubes.

Doc opened the door. The air was warm. Gnats mobbed the white light bulb outside the door. Far away, a truck bellowed on the highway.

He took his acoustic guitar and stepped onto the walkway. He pulled the door shut and went around to the back of the motel. He found the stairway that led to the roof and climbed the two stories.

A thin layer of gravel covered the flat roof of the motel. His feet crunched on the pebbles like he was walking on cornflakes.

Behind the motel, the mountains cut a jagged black outline into the glow of stars. The moon shone on the face of the mountains, throwing black shadows of rocks and cliffs and scraggly pinon trees on the ground. The mountains eased into a rolling plain dotted with twinkling lights that declined gently into the Rio Grande valley. On the other side of the slow, muddy river, a dusting of light hung over Juarez.

The stars were dim in the flat horizon to the south, across the dome of the sky. Doc had read somewhere that some of the stars he saw no longer existed. They had burnt out long ago, but they had not yet gone dim to our eyes because of the time and distance the light had to travel. And sound traveled even slower. He wondered how long it would take the chords he had played in his lifetime to reach the nearest star, if there was any kind of life there to hear the sound once it arrived, if beings who finally hear the music would even understand the blues.

He pulled his fingers across an E chord, followed by an A7. What a phenomenal bunch of noise and energy we send into the sky, he thought. Radios and televisions and car engines and riots and gunshot and sirens and whistles and crickets and waterfalls and pots clanging and horns and gasps and hundreds of musical instruments and footsteps and thunderstorms. And voices. A huge gathering of voices laughing and yelling and arguing and sobbing. By the time all the sounds reached anywhere else it would be a massive blob of tones, completely meaningless, just like if you mix all the colors in the spectrum and you get black every time.

Black sound.

Dawn began to etch a subtle indigo-black sky beyond the window.

Doc chuckled. What a squawking planet we are. And here I am with my little guitar and its six strings, doing whatever I can with the little bit of sound I've got, thinking it might make a difference somehow, might even mean something. Maybe it does. Ike played, people listened, men and women went into the parking lots after Ike's show and made love in their cars. Doc grinned. Yes. He'd touched a few people with his guitar. He'd broken through the noise and made some music.

He played two more chords. The music bounced around the brick and cement and glass of the motel and its neighboring shops. He fingered one of the warmup scales Ike had taught him. He went to another. It had taken him a long time to figure out why Ike had made him do these exercises. When he first knew Ike, he thought the old guitarist simply was a stickler for form, a traditionalist who pushed the ABCs at the cost of creativity. The old man insisted on the goddamnest rudimentary stuff. Now, Doc understood. The exercises taught him discipline, but they also gave his fingers the strength and independence to explore beyond the written boundaries. The monotonous repetition had confined him at first, but it ultimately freed him, because he could set his fingers in motion on a certain musical course, knowing they would do what they were supposed to do while he loosed his mind to invent new paths.

Doc's fingers followed a meandering blues, his right hand picking out a lead verse that alternated with backup chords, the fingers of his left hand moving from note to note with the precision of struck typewriter keys, while his mind wandered across the memories of his life – the life with painted women and pissy bars and dying cars and scarred highways and one-room apartments with electric lights that fizzled when you switched them on. There was an army of musicians wandering in and out of Doc's life, pill-dropping drummers, drunken sax players, piano players with steaming cigarettes poked in the corners of their mouths, female singers in sparkling gowns and breast-loose blouses strutting tiny stages with microphones held to their lips, hip young bass players who moved on to the coastal cities, worn

151

old horn players who hung onto the scene with wives who worked day jobs and came out on Friday and Saturday nights to root for their men in the jazz clubs and taverns where the drunks and loners and lovers of blues and jazz gather.

Doc walked to the edge of the roof and looked out over the city. He pulled his fingers across the strings and sent a spray of blues down onto the street. He always marveled at the tone and character of the acoustic guitar, the resonance in the wood, the quiet, fluid beauty of the chords.

Doc perched on the gravel roof of the motel and played until the pre-dawn light traced a 'blue line along the eastern horizon. Then, he lay the guitar down and practiced one of the first exercises Ike had taught him: He listened to the morning sounds, the birds that nested in the cement and bricks, chirping lightly as the stars began to fade.

Sporadic automobiles motored along the street. He looked down at the street that was gray and still, a slow concrete river pushing through a dawny plain. Headlights bobbed along the dips of the road in the distance, disappearing and coming back, poking through the blue-gray air like blinking, waking eyes.

Footsteps sounded on the pavement. A man carrying a white plastic bag rummaged among the trash bins. He checked the edge of the parking lot, found a pop can and stuffed it into his bag.

Across the street, a bird hopped along the sidewalk, seeking bits of bread, popcorn, garbage.

Doc lifted his arm and pulled his hand across the strings hard, jarring the morning with his blues.

The bird stopped and stood on one leg. The bag man straightened his back and listened. Everything was quiet for a moment as the guitar chord faded away.

Doc stood on the edge of the roof looking out at the dusty morning city and gave a bow.

About the Author

Steve Hallock, director of the graduate program in the School of Communication at Point Park University in Pittsburgh, has published six previous books, including the novel *The Silent Treatment*; a memoir of the '60s, *In Cheesman Park*; and a true-crime book about the solving of a 30-year-old cold case involving the murder of a young woman during the 1970s in Western Pennsylvania, *Justice Delayed*. A Denver native, he is a former jazz critic for *The Arizona Republic* in Phoenix and a writer for *The Albuquerque Journal*. He has published commentary in newspapers that include *The New York Times*, *Pittsburgh Post-Gazette*, *Denver Post*, and *Philadelphia Inquirer*. He and his wife, Joanne, live in Mount Lebanon, PA.